A Witch's Night Out

By

Tara Quan

Featuring:

Flirting with Fire
Frosty Relations
Fireworks at Midnight

CB

Decadent Publishing
www.decadentpublishing.com

This book is a work of fiction. Names, characters, places, and incidents are the products of the author's imagination or used fictitiously. Any resemblance to actual events, locales or persons, living or dead, is entirely coincidental.

A Witch's Night Out
Copyright 2015 by Tara Quan
ISBN: 978-1-61333-787-5
Cover design by Tibbs Designs

Published by Decadent Publishing Company
www.decadentpublishing.com

Printed in the United States of America

FLIRTING WITH FIRE

Chapter One

*L*eonardo Difuoco stared at the sleek, short-haired black cat stretched out on his white kitchen tiles. Crouching, he placed an open can of tuna-flavored Friskies on the floor. "Come on. Give it a shot. It's the highest rated brand on PetSmart.com."

The feline's emerald-green eyes narrowed. She yawned and twitched her whiskers from side to side. Before he'd inherited this house and the damn cat from his great-aunt, he hadn't realized an animal's face could express emotions like boredom and annoyance. He'd since learned the species bore a remarkable resemblance to humans.

"Work with me, Cat." He stood, crossed his arms, and invoked his most serious courtroom voice. "I can't keep making you breakfast. I subsisted on protein bars until you came along, and spending twenty minutes every morning to whip up eggs and sausage doesn't fit my schedule. I understand Nonna's dying depressed you, but it's been six months. Every other cat eats Friskies."

His silent-conversation partner curled onto her feet, lifted her butt, curved her back, and swiped the can with her right paw. The container crashed into the wall, its contents flying in all directions. With one last over-the-shoulder glance at him, the destructive housemate from hell loped off. As far as messages went, he'd received this one loud and clear.

"Talk about high maintenance." He scooped up the mess and dumped it into the trash bin. Then he took out a bottle of diluted bleach, sprayed the tiles, and sanitized the area. This burst of bad behavior added to his growing list of gripes. Though the beast didn't have much fur, he'd spotted random hairs all over the house. The little demon seemed to have an ax to grind. She targeted his furniture when sharpening her claws, leaving the few remaining mahogany mammoths he'd inherited from his departed great-aunt in pristine condition. Thank God for the self-cleaning litter box. The white cylindrical machine seemed to require no maintenance, and he hadn't caught a whiff of pee in the past six months.

His father, a first-generation Italian immigrant and staunch Catholic, was a stickler for spotless surroundings. His mother had loved her cranky borderline OCD engineer enough to adapt to his meticulous ways. For his sake, she'd minimized contact with her eccentric, cat-obsessed Romani family. With her husband's severe psychological allergy to dirt and dander, any visits to homes with pets had been out of the question.

Along with black hair, blue eyes, and a complexion so pale he suffered from sunburn at the slightest provocation, Leo had inherited his forbear's particularities when it came to cleanliness. Not once in his twenty-seven-year existence had owning a pet crossed his mind. For reasons he couldn't fathom, his mother's aunt's dying wish had been for him to take care of her cat, to whom the old bat had bequeathed half of everything she'd owned. Her request made little sense, considering he'd not once set foot in this house prior to owning it. He'd run into Nonna a few times at funerals and weddings, at which his father had insisted they spend as little time as possible. But since she'd left him several hundred thousand dollars in assets and property in addition to guardianship of her pet, adhering to the terms of her will seemed the honorable path.

And, to be honest, the cat, who was also named Cat, more or less took care of herself, aside from the whole not-eating business. It'd taken him over a month to notice the level of pet food in the automatic dispenser never decreased, after which he'd tempted her with human fare. Breakfast food, cake, and chocolate seemed to do the trick. Even though she appeared far from malnourished, he couldn't stand the thought of the old girl being hungry. He'd become accustomed to her greeting him when he came home, even if it was with a distracted meow. Besides, a bit of cushy padding made her more pleasant to hold, and having a green-eyed black cat curled up on his lap added a whole new dimension to slumming on the couch with an episode of *Supernatural*.

Cat chose this moment to return. Plunking down her plush bottom with her front legs straight and her heart-shaped face tilted up, the little minx stared up at him with a comical approximation of puppy-dog eyes. "Meow."

Keeping a straight face took significant effort. "Feeling guilty, are you?"

Those uncanny eyes grew even wider, her long, dark tail wagging in a slow, hypnotizing pattern. He found his muscles relaxing, all tension and anger melting away. Unnerved by the almost-magical effect, he picked the creature up and held her in front of his face. "Your little tricks won't work on me. I'm not letting you get off so easily. What you did was very rude."

Her claws sheathed, she batted at his nose with one paw. "Meeeow."

His resolve melted. He'd grown soft over the past six months, and the damn cat had learned to use it to her advantage. "Fine. I accept your apology. Now, run along. I need to wash up and get ready for work."

When he set her down, she padded after him to the master bedroom, which he'd refurnished as soon as he moved in. Aside from not wanting to sleep in his great-aunt's bed, the gothic decor had given him the creeps. What kind of old Italian-Gypsy used black sheets and installed a massive upturned crescent moon as her headboard? The memory of the blood-red carpet, emblazoned with weird black spirals, circles, and stars, still made him shudder.

He'd banished everything from the room, including a wall-sized, cross-bisected circular mirror, several dozen candles in all shapes, sizes, and colors, and multiple bouquets of odd-smelling herbs to the Salvation Army. He'd no clue what they'd do with it all, but he liked clean, sleek lines and modern furniture too much to have such bizarre items in his house.

Cat had been none too happy with his decision. Her housewarming presents were claw marks on every corner of his bed's leather base. The rest of his furniture, including his chrome desk, rolling ergonomic office chair, and black IKEA chest of drawers all met with similar fates. To his relief, the feline soon grew tired of vandalism and started bothering him in other ways.

Accompanying him into the bathroom was a good example. While unaffectionate, the cat never ventured more than a few feet away. She had the decency to stay outside until the shower came on, but the sound of cascading water seemed to act as a trigger. Within seconds of him rinsing off, her sleek dark head would poke into the stall. His great-aunt must have installed some weird hi-tech cat sensor on all the internal doors. The creature roamed every nook and cranny of the three-story brownstone as if locks didn't exist.

Testing his limits must be on today's agenda since a black streak crossed his line of vision before he could shut the bathroom door. Already behind schedule, he crouched and jabbed his forefinger between his pet's green eyes. "You know the drill. No coming in until after I strip."

In lieu of an answer, she jumped to sit on the new granite sink. Unlike his furniture reshuffle, Cat had no beef with his bathroom and kitchen remodels. His stainless steel appliances, copper fixtures, and terra-cotta tiles all escaped the wrath of her claws.

Rising, he swept his arm toward the open entryway. "I don't have time for this. Out you go. I mean it." When his stern warning failed to achieve the desired effect, he heaved a sigh. Past experience taught him a chase almost never ended in capture.

Not bothering to close off the room, he hooked his fingers under his boxers' waistband. "You're a little pervert. Can't you at least act like you're not looking?" Very few sane people had lengthy conversations with their pets. He needed to get a life.

His audience of one lay down on her stomach, her face resting on her paws. The first couple of months, she'd pretended to be interested in something else—his assortment of fluffy white towels, for example. Now, she watched him shower like it was nobody's business. Sighing, he took off his shorts and tossed them into the hamper, his aim perfect enough to remind him of his basketball-playing days. She meowed and nodded, as if in approval.

He stepped into the glass enclosure, feeling oddly self-conscious. With a twist of the handle, water fell like rain over his head. As he scrubbed, he continued to address the cat. "I'm going out tonight. It's Halloween, and the guys are beginning to think I've turned into a hermit."

The ensuing meow was pitched higher than usual. Though he hesitated to read too much into feline noises, his brain somehow interpreted the sound as an expression of enthusiasm. The plan he'd been lukewarm about gained appeal. "Besides, costume parties are great places to pick up chicks."

He cringed at a loud crash. Poking his head out, he took stock of the damage. Ceramic shards from what used to be his soap holder covered the floor, along with globs of shiny translucent liquid. His fingers itched to take care of the mess, but his schedule dictated he leave the task to his daily housekeeper.

His destructive cat sat with her back facing him, her tail forming a perfect C.

"Careful. I'm beginning to think you're jealous."

He heard a low growl over the din of falling water.

Shutting the shower off, he stepped onto the miraculously unscathed bathmat and patted himself dry. The cat continued to face the wall. "You're grouchy because a special episode of

Supernatural airs tonight, right? Don't worry. I've already set the DVR. We'll watch it together, tomorrow."

She remained silent, but her tail twitched.

"It's not like I'll get lucky. Whenever I bring someone home, weird shit happens and gets in the way. You wouldn't have anything to do with it, would you?" Crazy to blame the cat, but his gut insisted she triggered all the surreptitious ends to his dates, perhaps because she never failed to leave claw marks on his guests' shoes.

After a prolonged back stretch, she pivoted to face him. The slow lip lick accompanying her smug expression did little to alleviate his suspicions.

A towel wrapped around his waist, he scooted around the danger zone and preceded her to the walk-in Container Store-outfitted closet. Padding about the house naked with the cat trailing him felt weird, an illogical reaction since she watched him shower on a regular basis. He should be used to her by now. She fell asleep next to him on the couch almost every night. He'd made a conscious decision not to install a television in the bedroom, thinking it might deter him from indulging too much in the pastime, but his penchant for dozing off on the oversized leather sofa in the living room dashed all hope of kicking his TV habit.

Pulling on a starched, French-cuffed white shirt, he made a mental note to give the maid a raise. The woman had called his office soon after he moved in and told him she'd been cleaning his great-aunt's house for the past three years. Since she already had a set of keys and charged a reasonable fee, they worked out a system where he left her week's wages on the kitchen island every Monday. He also created a shared Amazon account, so she could order cleaning supplies and nonperishable food items online.

He never returned home in time to meet the lady, who happened to have a remarkably sexy voice. But she kept the house in tip-top shape, his pantry well stocked, and saved him a small fortune in dry cleaning. Although she refused to go out to shop for groceries, she always combined his hodgepodge of edible items into microwave-ready meals. He found the shopping lists she left him very helpful. Before she'd entered his life, he seemed incapable of remembering he preferred 2% milk in his cereal but whole milk for coffee.

In honor of Halloween, the pagan-festival-turned-consumerist American holiday, he shrugged on a black suit and looped an orange tie around his neck. A silver tie clip patterned with smiling jack-o'-lanterns completed the outfit. Fastening on a pair of bat-shaped cufflinks and matching them with socks bearing the same pattern, he jogged down the stairs.

Opening the entryway closet door, he took a moment to appreciate his collection of shiny, Italian-made lace-ups, all of which had stitched leather soles. His one battered pair of Nike sneakers created a bit of an eyesore, but he'd worn them in too well to buy something new.

Having followed him down, the cat sidled against the bottom of his trousers, leaving behind a furry trace. He'd figured out a while back why sticky lint brushes ranked among the top ten bestsellers on PetSmart.com. Removing the trail of hair almost on autopilot, he nudged the feline's head in the direction of his array of footwear. "What do you think? Black, dark brown, light brown, tan, or burgundy?"

She drew an infinity sign with her nose, which he'd long since decided was the feline equivalent of an eye roll. Nonetheless, she snaked through his legs and stopped in front of his plainest black pair.

He made a mental note to order a refill for the lint remover as he swiped at the loose hairs. "Come on, now. Not even wingtips?"

She lifted both front legs and placed her paws on the chosen shoe. Facing him, she purred.

"Talk about boring. Fine, I'll give you this one, since I'm leaving you alone tonight." Lacing up, he cast his gaze around in search of his briefcase.

Cat jumped onto the kitchen island, rubbing against the

black leather attaché.

"You're a mind reader." He rose from his crouch and grabbed it. "Okay, off I go."

A meow prompted him to halt. He swiveled around to find the cat on the small table in the foyer where he'd left his keys and wallet. Patting her on the head, he stuffed both into his pocket. "What would I do without you?"

☙

The moment the door clicked shut behind her boss, Catalina Gato shifted into her natural human form. Twisting the dead bolt into place, she shook her head. The man took forever to get out of the house. As much as she appreciated high-quality eye candy, she had better things to do with her morning.

She sniffed her sweaty T-shirt and winced. The clueless warlock had returned home earlier than usual yesterday afternoon, obliterating her window of opportunity to rinse off. Even though she'd spent their entire time together as a cat, she found staying in the same clothes for over twenty-four hours beyond gross. Padding to the smallest guest bath on the third floor, she stripped and shuffled into the glass stall. Though not as nice as the massaging rainfall in the master, she preferred to shower here since Leo almost never wandered into this section of the house. His absence allowed her to leave toiletries out in the open and commandeer the closet in the adjoining bedroom to store her stuff.

After a near miss early in their cohabitation, when he'd come home to grab some lunch while she was washing her hair, she'd decided to maintain a strict his-zone her-zone rule. His epic sense of denial somehow made him not question why a cat had streaked out of his bathroom sopping wet, but she'd rather not take any chances.

Rubbing shampoo into her chin-length black hair, she contemplated her options. Since tonight was All Hallows' Eve, she had twelve hours of absolute freedom. At sunset, she'd gain the ability to leave this damn house and not risk morphing into a cat if she somehow ventured within ten feet of her master. She could embrace the holiday spirit and go out for a night on the town, or she could track down the bumbling new owner of her contract and tell him the truth.

Though any familiar would describe her situation as unsustainable, she would hate to break her promise to her departed mentor, Nonna the Great. But she'd given the woman's great-nephew six months to come around, and he was no closer to accepting his magical side. Because he had no inkling he was a warlock, he couldn't formalize his status as her master. This made it impossible for him to give her express permission to reveal her human form, take vacation days other than Halloween, or leave his domain.

To think she'd been thrilled when his great-aunt offered her this five-year apprenticeship. Euphoric from getting her first job offer, she'd spared the clauses on the enchanted roll of parchment no more than a second's glance before signing it in blood. After all, any self-respecting elemental witch or warlock would perform the ritual allowing a full renegotiation of terms prior to the beginning of service, as Nonna had done within seconds of hiring her. The physical contract, along with all the pesky antiquated codicils, served as a reminder of times past—a tradition borne out of nostalgia and the Wiccan flair for theatrics.

For this reason, she'd found out about the service transferring to the witch's heir upon death *after* her previous master had died. In hindsight, she should have studied the terms of her apprenticeship in greater detail, seeing as how the woman had been approaching a hundred at the time of her interview. But Cat's eagerness to tell her parents she'd escaped the menacing clutches of post-graduation unemployment led to uncharacteristic carelessness, and the momentary lapse in judgment went on to bite her in the ass.

She could have asked her family to help appeal the case when Nonna passed, but Cat had promised the old crone she'd take care of "her dear little *nipote,* Leo," who turned out to be a twenty-seven-year-old intellectual property attorney with a deep-seated rejection of the occult. Of course, she should have seen the signs. Nonna's estranged niece never visited, and in all the framed pictures that had once graced the living room mantle, the image of Leo's father had been scorched out. If the previous owner of this house were to be believed, Difuoco, Sr. had been a "sanctimonious *coglione*" who'd isolated his wife and son from their magical roots with a methodical fanaticism that approached madness. This uncanny ability to ignore glaring evidence of the supernatural seemed to be a trait his son inherited.

Her new boss's denial of magic was so entrenched, his subconscious sabotaged all her attempts to enlighten him to his true nature. What should have been a simple matter of leaving him a note became a major fire hazard as paper, parchment, cloth, his laptop, and even a painted wall went up in flames as soon as he glimpsed her messages out of the corner of his eye. To make matters worse, he'd chalked up his haywire explosive bursts of power to the old house's bad wiring and used it as an excuse to remodel.

And, thus, her charming witch's den full of antique furniture, flying carpets, and invaluable artifacts devolved into a bachelor pad, sparsely furnished, with a 60-inch plasma screen, which she rather appreciated, several gaming consoles, IKEA dressers, and more leather surfaces than any house should contain.

Her failure to communicate with the dratted man resulted in six months of house arrest. A familiar was the Energizer Bunny to an elemental witch or warlock's battery pack. While in animal form, they stored up pure energy, which could be used by their employer to perform more complex enchantments and spells. Familiars also had the discretion to channel stockpiled mojo into less-advanced but useful witchery most elementals considered beneath them. Without her, Leo couldn't access his power in any form other than its most basic state, which might have been helpful back in the days when starting fires took a lot of effort. In the twenty-first century, such magic was more an inconvenience than anything else, which was why shape-shifting witches such as Cat still earned a living wage.

Since familiars processed energy most efficiently by staying in non-human form while in close proximity with their masters, the outdated boilerplate Familiar Employment Agreement included a clause preventing the contracted parties from assuming their natural state without express permission. It also confined them to two physical locations: the contract holder's domicile or a ten-foot radius around their person. Since indentured servitude had been made illegal over a hundred years before, both these archaic clauses were almost always waived via a simple ritual.

But because the person who inherited her contract didn't have a clue magic existed, he hadn't uttered the incantation permitting her to revert to her natural form. Forced to appear to him as a cat until otherwise indicated, she couldn't explain her need for more than a single twelve-hour holiday a year, which had been the modus operandi back in the Dark Ages, when the contract language was first drafted. In keeping with modern employment practices, Nonna had given her all the Federal holidays off, in addition to a handful of sick days and casual leave.

If the stupid warlock wasn't such a homebody, she might have been able to stick it out. A well-established young professional in his prime should go out more. His attachment to hearth and home exceeded his great-aunt's, which said something about his lack of a social life. He adhered to a strict work-gym-house routine and seemed to prefer couch surfing to drinking at a bar. Her *me-time* dwindled even further when he cancelled his gym membership and converted Nonna's old spell nook into a workout room. As much as she enjoyed watching the man pump iron, the all-look-and-no-play situation wreaked havoc on her already crazy libido.

Soaping her too-sensitive body, she closed her eyes and recalled an image of him from earlier that morning. She'd wanted nothing more than to slip through the glass doors, run her palms along those wet, chiseled abs, and trace the defined lines of chest muscle with her fingers. After less than two minutes of voyeurism, she'd imagined levering herself using those broad shoulders, wrapping her legs around his torso, and fusing her mouth with his.

Why did her boss have to be clueless *and* sexy? If not for the latter trait, it'd be much easier to hate his guts. Instead, she was trapped in a weird limbo between impatient annoyance and unbridled horniness. She switched the water to a cold blast. It didn't help.

One cardinal rule existed in all professions—*Thou shalt not lust after the boss*. To it, she'd add—*especially not when you're his minion, bound by blood to do his bidding, and he doesn't see you as a human being*. But the impracticality of this attraction didn't change the fact this man appealed to her in the most carnal way. It was a good thing she transformed into a cat whenever he came close, else her panties would be damp from constant sexual fantasies.

When she slept, she dreamt of learning the texture of his dark five o'clock shadow with her lips, of feeling his coarse chest hair rasp over her breasts. He might be no more than two inches taller than her, but she'd be powerless in his grasp. The man was all muscle, from his thick neck to his toned arms. Even without the magical rules demanding her complete obedience, he could compel her to do whatever he wanted.

This embarrassing and unrelenting lust put an impetus on finding a way out. She'd served Nonna for a little over three years and spent the past six months in his care, leaving an interminable eighteen months on the damn contract. By the time it ended, she'd be a frustrated nymphomaniac.

Rinsing the last of the suds, she shut off the shower and stepped out. After wiping away the condensation, she stared at her reflection in the mirror. Heat and arousal had combined to bring a blush to her cheeks, turning her amber complexion close to orange. Rivulets of water dripped from her short-cropped hair and dotted her neck and chest, which rose and fell with each shallow pant. For no reason she could fathom, her lips glowed bright red.

She needed to get hold of herself. Her neck and cleavage were damp with sweat despite the recent shower. Her breasts ached, her nipples tightening into sharp buds. She closed her hands over the full mounds, her grasp too small to provide any relief. A memory of Leo's long fingers rushed to the fore. She could feel his calluses over her skin, imagine those strong hands milking her flesh. Desire gathered deep within, the molten throb prompting her to flatten her palms on the mirror.

Filling her lungs with steamy air, she forced her rampant imagination under control. Tonight was All Hallows' Eve—her contractually mandated holiday. She needed to decide what to do with those liberating twelve hours, not fantasize about the one man she should never make a move on.

Chapter Two

"*What* do you mean, I shouldn't confront him?" Cat gaped at her little sister's image on the computer screen. "You've been egging me on to take another stab for months."

"Shelley has a vibe. You need to do something else tonight." Dulcina thrived as a familiar to her childhood best friend, elemental witch-in-training Shelley Dupree. Thick as thieves since they attached their hips to each other on the first day of daycare, the two made one of the oddest Wiccan pairs. Their arrangement more a partnership than an apprenticeship, they cohabited a small townhouse in northern Virginia, two Metro stops from the city-center brownstone Cat shared with Leo in the District of Columbia.

Her confidence shaken, she nonetheless protested, "I won't take life advice from someone who's too young to buy alcohol. Besides, didn't you tell me *your friend's* visions," she drew quotes in the air with her fingers, "are hit or miss?"

As an earth witch, Shelley should have minimal non-elemental powers, making her frequent accurate premonitions suspect. Cat had long since pegged her sister as the source of all these predictions. Because the girl insisted on staying in the precognition closet, hinting at the truth was an effective way to get under her skin.

Dulcina, who preferred the nickname Sweets due to repeated

shortening of her given name to some variation of Douche, Douchy, or China, refused to take the bait. "*Shelley's* vibes are always spot on. That said, they're too vague to be useful most of the time."

"Bringing us back to...."

Sweets lifted an eyebrow. "Remember what happened to the wall you painted with your cockamamie message? By the way, big sis, couldn't you come up with anything better than 'You're a warlock, and I'm your familiar'?"

The surface had gone up in flames, leaving sooty black scorch marks requiring an expensive paint job that resulted in the entire interior going from invigorating crimson to boring dove gray. "I'm not an inanimate object."

"Which means you'll die if this goes wrong. Are you willing to risk your life for freedom?"

As much as she hated to admit it, the answer was no. A decade of liberty might be worth it, but not a year and a half. "I can't stay like this for much longer. Do you want to see me as an ill-behaved, tantrum-throwing lunatic?" Sweets nodded, prompting Cat to narrow her eyes. "I'm cooped up indoors alone all day and spend the rest of my time as a cat. I haven't bothered to wear anything but T-shirts and pajama bottoms in six months. This is the worst job on the planet."

Her sister scratched her pointed nose. "Even compared to the child laborers jobs, slaving away while locked inside a Chinese factory?"

Cat wasn't in the mood for a whose-life-is-crappier debate. "Okay, the worst excuse for an apprenticeship. I can't learn magic from someone who doesn't practice it. What's the point of my being here?"

Sweets lifted her hand and rubbed her thumb over the tips of her fingers. "Since Mamá steamrolled you into burying your recent windfall in retirement accounts and long-term mutual funds, your end-of-service bonus lets you go on that world tour you've been harping on about. And who knows? I might need you to bail my broke ass out of trouble some time in the next twenty years. It's important you have as much accessible cash as possible."

"Your future lack of funds," Cat gritted out, "is not more important than my professional development."

"Oh, please. You've learned plenty. Familiars channel a witch's raw power to do practical mundane enchantments. Haven't you been doing nothing but those for the past six months? I'd bet you tried something new and awesome today."

Best not admit she'd returned a broken soap holder to its original state less than an hour before, a feat she'd pulled off for the first time. "My goal in life is *not* to be a warlock's maid. I spend all day playing Zumba in front of the Xbox and cleaning the place. Lack of dust is one of the few things in life the man cares about."

"Don't be so melodramatic." Sweets rolled her eyes. "Your booty's less flabby, thanks to all the exercise, and it's not like you've ever held a mop. You cast spells on all the cleaning supplies, and they work on autopilot, which, by the way, is some high-level voodoo shit. Do you see Shelley, or me, or even Mamá pulling off those types of stunts? No, we're stuck moving our own brooms around."

The longer she remained a cat, the more magic she had to command. Since she spent fourteen hours a day, on average, amassing her boss's energy, she was capable of some very impressive work. "My fat butt and cleaning excellence is not the point. I'm approaching twenty-five. I should be doing something more meaningful with my life."

"I'd trade my trim waistline for your 'fat' ass, and don't go adding to your age. You've two years before you hit the big two-five. And what have you ever wanted to be besides a familiar?"

Nothing, which was why she'd jumped at the chance to pair up with Nonna. "You and your skinny one hundred pounds don't have to size up so everything fits around the chest and hips. And I'm not much of a familiar, since my warlock isn't aware I exist. Even if he were, I'm better at magic than he is."

Sweets waved her hand, the motion creating a pixelated blur

on the video feed. "He knows you exist, just not as a person. Trust me, there are plenty of other personal assistants in D.C. who share similar fates."

Cat crossed her arms. "Familiars aren't personal assistants."

"You've been drinking too much Wiccan Kool-Aid. If you had read your contract, which would have prevented these less than desirable circumstances from occurring, you'd agree with me. The whole point of our existence is so the almighty hocus-pocus crowd can focus on big-picture stuff and not have to deal with life's inconveniences."

Cat narrowed her eyes. Her sister was equal parts blunt and insightful, an exasperating combination. "Why did you sign a contract with Shelley if you're so against the arrangement?"

Sweets batted her eyelashes. "Aside from her being my BFF and so clueless she needs constant supervision?"

If her sister ever bothered to ask Cat's opinion, she'd tell Sweets her witch deserved more credit despite suffering from the magical equivalent of agoraphobia. "My point is, you two have an equal footing in the partnership. As far as Leo's concerned, I might as well not be here."

Her sister counted off on her fingers. "Let's see...you manage the man's financial portfolio, pay his bills, do his taxes, keep his house dust-free and shiny. In your spare hours, you make sure he's fed, wakes up on time to go to work, and doesn't miss an episode of *Supernatural*. Trust me, if you disappeared, he'd notice."

Cat took a deep breath. "No one wants to spend all day picking index funds and managing people's books."

"Umm.... I think those who do that are called accountants and financial advisors. Didn't you get a bachelors in something along those lines?"

Cat was a CPA and broker with a degree in finance and accounting. To supplement her salary, she managed the portfolios of multiple clients online. Though her foresight didn't compare to the Sweets-Shelley duo, combining the latent ability with a good grasp of current events allowed for a decent profit on the stock market.

Since this conversation had gone off on an odd tangent, Cat reverted to the original topic. "So, is there any other reason I shouldn't confront Leo tonight in a very visible public location and ask him to void my contract? Aside from the slim possibility of me bursting into flames?"

"I told you. Shelley's vibes point to a different path."

Cat massaged her temples. "Could you…? Did she give more details?"

Tapping sounds crackled over the speaker. A second later, an e-mail notification popped up. Cat opened it and frowned. "How does my going on a one-night stand solve anything? And isn't Madame Eve *the* matchmaker."

Sweets cleared her throat. "The whole soul mates thing is a marketing ploy. I'm not 100% sure how this invitation will solve all your problems, but I…. Shelley said your planets are about to come into alignment. She even prepaid for the service, and you know how stingy she is."

Such astrological events could be either fortuitous or disastrous, depending on the exact circumstances. "I don't see how—"

"You have the hots for your boss, and for some reason, you're convinced it's a problem. I don't understand what the big deal is, but maybe getting laid will give you the extra oomph to stick it out until your contract expires. There's a $50,000 bonus tied to the clause—hard-earned wages you'd earmarked to spend on yourself long before Nonna died, so there's a chance you won't buckle under parental pressure and squirrel it away. Until then, his home gym saves you a fortune on membership fees."

"I can't leave the apartment to exercise regardless…." But other than that, her sister had a point. How annoying. "And I don't feel like having sex." At least, not with anyone other than the boss in question.

"What's wrong with expanding your horizons? As nice as your ex-boyfriend Bobby was, the dork didn't even watch porn. Did you get off once during sex in the three years you were together, or did you have to crest the hill solo?"

"None of your business." The brat was too perceptive by half. "Besides, a one-night stand seems so...torrid."

Her sister's nose wrinkled. "What are you, some Victorian romance heroine? You've been spending too much time cooped up at home, reading Georgette Heyer. If it makes you feel any better, Shells assures me your life will change after tonight."

The problem with the word *change* was its neutrality. You could never tell with witches, young ones in particular. A premonition this vague could mean a serial killer planned to murder her. "So, you want me to spend my single holiday of the year meeting some stranger—"

"And having mind blowing orgasms? Hell, yes. It'll help relieve stress, and doesn't pose any risk of spontaneous combustion."

Conceding her point, Cat skimmed over the invitation. "It says here I'm supposed to meet my mystery date at the Castillo Capital Hotel at 7:00 p.m. for Masquerade Night. How am I supposed to get a Halloween costume on such short notice?"

Her sister's triumphant smile exposed two rows of perfect white teeth. "According to UPS, the package I ordered for you was delivered yesterday."

Since she bought all nonperishable household items online, a small mountain of brown boxes sat on the kitchen island. Having a subscription for cereal said something about her impending insanity. "I'm not going to like it at all, am I?"

"Don't be silly. It's perfect for you. Go open it and see."

੧੩

Averting his gaze from the bedraggled ten-year-old folder containing what might one day be an approved patent application, Leo watched his best friend drop into a rolling office chair. Seated on the opposite side of his desk, Jackson Frost III leaned back and swung his legs in the air. Missing the edge by an inch on the way down, he nonetheless achieved a half-recline. A paralegal had deposited a tall stack of binders on the carpet this morning, so it didn't take much brainpower to deduce the current location of those shiny lace-ups. If it had been anyone else, the offensive transfer of dirt would have prompted immediate eviction. But since their friendship spanned a decade, Leo gritted his teeth and let the transgression slide.

Picking up the invitation that had been tossed onto his desk, he read it out loud. "Madame Eve cordially invites you to a one-night stand. Please meet your mystery date at the Castillo Capital Hotel for Masquerade Night at 7:00 p.m. A Halloween costume and mask is highly recommended." He set the thick piece of vellum down. "You must be joking."

"I have a strict budget for jokes, and this setup wasn't cheap." The firm's most notorious spendthrift laced his hands behind his blond head. "Happy twenty-eighth, old man."

"Dude, I'm not sleeping with a hooker. Not even a pre-paid hooker."

His friend's brows lifted, the pasty-white face morphing into a comical facsimile of affront. "It's 'Madame Eve' not 'Madam Eve.' The French use it as a term of respect, and she doesn't run an escort service. My gift to you is a genuine no-strings-attached one-night stand with who I assume will be a hot chick."

With a dismissive grunt, Leo tossed the card into the empty trash can. "Why?"

"Why what?"

"Why do you think the woman will be hot?"

Reaching down, Jack retrieved the invitation, and placed it back on the desk. "Madame Eve's service has received multiple accolades...."

"From whom?"

"Don't get all lawyerly on me. I have it on good authority you'll have a good time—let's leave it at that. Lighten up, will you? All the secretaries call you 'the comma Hitler.' Get that stick out of your butt."

Leo had never understood why insisting work be done to his exact specifications, on time and free of typos, had earned him a reputation as a domineering hard-ass. "I bet all you've done is read half a dozen Internet reviews. Did you even get past the star rating to see what people wrote?"

His persistent benefactor's comeback was enunciated in what no one would consider an inside voice. "Do you think there are user comments for this shit? Roll with it, okay? Haven't you been complaining about lack of action? How long has this dry spell been—six months? Time to get back on the horse."

Raising his gaze to the ceiling, he fought for patience. While he'd gained maturity and a hint of *ennui* by the tail end of his late twenties, his pal seemed to have regressed to an early-pubescent mental stage. "I don't have a problem securing dates. You've been my wingman too many times to say otherwise. But I'm pickier now. If I don't like the woman while at the bar, I don't ask her to spend the night. If I bring her home and it feels wrong, I don't go through with it."

"Uh-huh. *Pickiness* is your problem." An exaggerated nod accompanied the retort. "I was around the other day when you complained about your aunt's cat cock-blocking you."

There had been a grain of truth to the statement. Ever since he moved in with Cat, mustering the enthusiasm to close the deal had become impossible, regardless of the hotness rating of the date in question. "You try fooling around with someone while a cat stares at you, its whiskers twitching in judgment." Maybe he did sound a little insane.

"You can't deny you're in a slump when you're blaming your pet each time you crash and burn. It's not the cat's fault. All you need to do is lock it in the bathroom."

Confining the cat to any part of the house had no effect. Of course, if he voiced this observation, he'd sound even crazier. "Since when is my sex life your problem?"

"Since you blew me off for the hundredth time." At long last, he revealed the motivation behind this bizarre gift. "All you do is stay home, watch TV, buy new furniture, pick bathroom tiles, and figure out why the damn cat isn't eating. You even cancelled your gym membership. I need my spotter back." Aside from being the managing partner's son, his friend's professional success resulted from unabashed selfishness.

"I told you, it makes more sense to buy the machines than to pay over a hundred bucks a month to use a bunch of gross ones. People don't always wipe after they sweat." Wincing at the thought, he continued, "And I've been cutting down on my beer intake. With thirty around the corner, my metabolism is slowing."

His perpetually lean workout partner snorted. "The things some men do for vanity. Cut loose for one night and get your mojo back, will ya? I even paid for a hotel room—the sex-toy-equipped No Dreams Required suite. If this doesn't work, then we'll have to repeat our trip to Amsterdam this Thanksgiving."

While he'd learned quite a few new tricks and eaten some interesting baked goods during the spring break in question, the thought of repeating it left him bored and tired. "If you're right, and this woman isn't an escort, won't she slap me in the face as soon as she sees the setup?"

"If she's so prudish, count yourself lucky for escaping her clutches. Besides, this is a legit hotel, not a BDSM club. With the steep discount from Priceline, I'd be surprised if they're giving you more than condoms, lube, and a pair of handcuffs."

One of the firm's partners walked past their door, angled her head in their direction, and glared at them for a long moment before continuing forward. *Great.* This conversation improved by the minute. He lowered his voice in a not-so-subtle hint to his conversation partner. "This is a shit-load of effort, and you're the opposite of altruistic. Can't you make new friends or something?" Despite the man's tendency to be blunt and abrasive, he wouldn't describe his friend as a bad guy.

"I've already put too much work into us." Jack drew a circle in the air with his index finger. "High School. College. Law School. I'm counting a lot of years here, and I won't lose you to a fucking cat." An intern pushing a file cart ambled by the office, her gait slowing to a crawl as she passed. Glancing in her direction, the manipulative bastard rose, positioned himself in full view of the doorway, and continued in an even louder voice. "Get your dick in gear, my friend. It's time it sees some action. When everything's functioning down there, maybe you'll show me some love." As if the inappropriate statement weren't enough, he grabbed his own crotch and made a pumping motion with his hips.

A paralegal poked her head out of a cubicle. A loud crash echoed from the direction the file-cart had disappeared, followed by a muffled curse. Tempted to grab his friend by the shirt collar and duct tape his mouth shut, Leo warned, "Keep your voice down. Our admin staff gossips like there's no tomorrow. I'm going to get an e-mail from Human Resources any moment now."

"And what's the mousy little thing going to do, stammer at you to death?" A low hum of murmuring female voices followed the insult. "If anyone needs a one-night stand, it's her."

Since his single other option was to engage in a shouting match, he lifted his hands, palms up, in surrender. "If I promise to think about this invitation, will you shut up and leave?"

"Talk about a low-ball offer. Can we skip to the part where you promise me you'll show up at the restaurant tonight?" A smug grin accompanied the question.

He made one last-ditch effort to worm his way out. "It says I need a costume. I don't have one."

The invitation was launched into the air, landing on his lap. "Recommended isn't the same as required. I'll send my secretary out to buy you one of those *Phantom of the Opera* masks at Walgreens—and maybe a few condoms, while she's at it. Those are for me, not for you. You should get your own. A dozen or so."

This time, the eavesdropping paralegal stepped out of her cubicle and marched in the direction of the HR office. "I'm pretty sure Courtney prefers the title administrative assistant, and I think we're about to be fired."

"Please. My dad owns this company. I can also tell you Mr. Scrooge cares about one thing—billings. Since we both went over the minimum for this quarter, Ms. Mouse can tut-tut me all she wants."

He cleared his throat. "It's Ms. Mao."

"I'm well aware. Since it gets her panties in a twist, I'm making up random names. I'm hoping one will stick, but the pencil skirts in the cubicle pool refuse to cooperate. So, are you ready to commit yet, or should I start discussing porn?"

He hadn't been given much of a choice. Lifting the invite, he slid it into his briefcase. "If she's lame, I'm bailing. And you'd better not be lurking in some corner dressed up as Draco Malfoy."

"Who the heck is Draco Malfoy? A vegetarian vampire tween sensation or something?"

After over a decade of friendship, Leo had learned to recognize genuine confusion. How the man had obtained an engineering degree while staying immune to anything dorky was one of life's greatest mysteries. "He's the platinum-blond bully in *Harry Potter*. Do a Google images search."

"Why would you think I'd spy on your date?"

He managed to rescue his favorite blue pen before it made its way off his desk and into the grasping meddler's hand. "Because you always do."

"No need to get testy. I can tell you right now I wouldn't in a million years dress up as a wimpy wizard."

Which meant he should resign himself to having the most conspicuous voyeur imaginable. "Remind me—why are we friends?"

"Isn't it obvious?" A mock pout turned Jack's face almost angelic. "I balance you out—keep you off the straight and narrow."

Before he could come up with a retort, his phone trilled. Glancing at the caller ID, he pulled out his top drawer, dug around for an aspirin, and steeled himself for a lecture from Human Resources.

Chapter Three

"*H*ave you been to The Cigar Lounge before, Mr. Difuoco?" Costumed as Gomez from *The Addams Family*, the mustached maître d' wore a gray-striped suit, skinny tie, and had an oiled comb-over.

Leo shook his head as he glanced around the dimly lit room. A boutique hotel with a view of the National Mall, the Castillo Capital made up for its intimate size with old-world luxury. With a burnished brass base and dripping crystals, an antique-looking chandelier provided a centerpiece for their opulent lobby, which projected an image of quiet efficiency despite the heavy foot traffic. Located not far from the entrance, The Cigar Lounge seemed transported from a bygone era. Mahogany paneling, sleek leather chairs, and the scent of unlit tobacco combined to make the small restaurant and bar classy without being pretentious. A cordoned-off smoking room, walled in with glass and furnished with plush sofas and armchairs, took up one large interior corner.

Forty or so patrons milled about the much larger non-smoking section. Noting the number of masked men wearing business suits, he breathed a sigh of relief. He should never have been concerned about his lack of costume. This was 6:45 p.m. in downtown D.C. Like him, most young professionals would have come straight from work.

The majority of guests loitered by the oval bar in the center of the lounge. Four bartenders wearing pirate costumes took orders from every direction. Most women held clear gothic-style dragon goblets containing colorful cocktails, while men chugged draft beer from pewter ale mugs bearing a similar design. Multiple standing tables surrounded the bar, and additional wait staff scurried about delivering drinks and taking orders.

Deeper inside the room, eight bay windows formed a semicircle around the main lounge area. Each housed an eating nook containing a candlelit table for two. Costumed couples already occupied seven of these quasi-private spaces.

Adjusting his white *Phantom of the Opera* mask, Leo replied, "No, this is my first time here. I believe my reservation is under Madame Eve."

The short, balding man smiled. "Ah. Then you have an interesting night ahead of you. You're the first member of your party to arrive. Please, follow me."

Not long after, Leo sat at the remaining table, perusing a thick menu while sipping Blue Moon. Through the window, the carousel in front of the Smithsonian Castle spun. A horde of costumed children gathered on the lawn, their jack-o'-lantern baskets ready for candy. The National Mall served as an ideal meeting spot for trick-or-treaters intending to target the neighborhood behind Capitol Hill, where the most affluent movers-and-shakers dwelled. The trail ended at the historic Eastern Market up the road, which hosted an annual Halloween party many considered the city's best. As a young boy, he'd always thumbed through photos of costumed classmates with envy, never quite understanding why his father planned their family trip to Vatican City for the end of October every year.

He had to give Madame Eve credit. Even if his mystery date never showed up, he'd categorize this night as a pleasant experience. Arriving fifteen minutes before his reservation time, he'd had the opportunity to scope the place out. The hotel housed a number of expensive oil paintings and sculptures, and whoever had decorated the interior deserved an award. He couldn't wait to show Cat the photos he'd snapped on his phone. For some reason, the feline always gave him her undivided attention whenever he sorted through pictures on his computer, which was cute and freaky at the same time.

The BlackBerry he'd placed on the table lit up with an instant message.

J_Frost: *Y r chicks always L8?*

Leo lowered his menu. His seat allowed him a direct line of sight to the bar, where a certain platinum blond in a Hogwarts uniform stood ogling a buxom redhead. He couldn't figure out how Jack had found the costume so soon after their conversation, but he had to give the man credit. With his almost-white hair slicked back, he bore a striking resemblance to the *Harry Potter* character. Considering his messaging style, his friend might be a better fit for a magical high school than a grown-up lounge.

L_Difuoco: *Focus on your date.*

Less than a minute later, he received a response.

J_Frost: *Not d8. Random hot-e @ bar.*

It figured. Most women Jack spoke to for more than five minutes tended to never want to see him again.

L_Difuoco: *Then stop gawking at her boobs.*

J_Frost: *Y?*

His friend's brain wasn't wired to understand certain concepts, common decency and social norms among them. He'd discovered this truth many years back.

L Difuoco: *Higher chance of success.*

J_Frost: *Tru dat.... Speaking of ta-tas. Boobilicious Cat Chiquita @ ur 3 o'clock.*

The message diverted his attention to the entrance, where a masked female in a black leather bodysuit waited to be seated. She towered over the maître d', though her knee-high stiletto boots added at least four inches.

Gomez's manners thus far had been impeccable, but Leo could draw a straight line from the man's eyeballs to

Catwoman's chest. To be fair, those were some gorgeous breasts—either that or the woman wore a killer push-up bra. High, pert, and full, they combined with lush wide hips to form a perfect hourglass shape. In those heels, her legs seemed to go on for miles.

Distracted by the lithe yet voluptuous body, it took him a moment before he could focus on her face. She had straight, silky black hair, cut at the chin to form a short bob. Her dark leather mask started halfway down her forehead and ended under her cheekbone, lending her heart-shaped face a mysterious and sexy air. Plum red lipstick accentuated a pair of pouting lips, which were perfectly situated between a small button nose and sharp pointed chin.

He had to agree with Jack. Catwoman was smoking.

The maître d' led her into the lounge's interior. As she walked closer, her spicy perfume blended with the scent of fresh tobacco, the intoxicating combination interfering with his ability to focus. Spotting him, she stopped in her tracks.

Her emerald-green eyes went wide. Then she swept him from head to toe with her gaze. The direct scrutiny triggered a sudden tightness in his pants. An electric sizzle spread over his skin and made his fingertips tingle.

A collective gasp distracted him from the odd physiological reaction. The candle on his table now blazed blue instead of orange, the flame growing to twice its original size. He snuck a peek at the other tables, all of which seemed to be experiencing the same fiery effect.

The lounge must have invested in some fancy pyrotechnic candles in honor of Halloween.

Shrugging off the incident, he glanced back in time to see a smug smile on his future date's face. She stood in place and waited for the maître d' to collect himself. The man was a damn good actor. Wearing a stunned expression, he wiped the beads of sweat from his wrinkled forehead with a shaking hand.

As the person in charge, he must have been forewarned about the little trick. Maybe he hadn't realized when the stunt would go off.

A patron wearing a *Fantastic Four* Human Torch costume applauded, and soon everyone followed suit. Since her escort hadn't moved a muscle, Catwoman plucked the menu out of the man's trembling fingers and marched over to the table. "So there's no confusion, you're here for Madame Eve's one-night stand?" The end of her sentence lacked an upward inflection. As she spoke, her voice grew louder while the pitch lowered, making the statement seem more like an accusation than a simple request for clarification.

Leaning back in his chair, he raised a brow in challenge. "I'm guessing I'm a disappointment?"

He could see her eyes narrowing through her mask's cut-out holes. "More like something fishy is going on. Did you sign up for the service yourself?"

An odd question. His gaze automatically drifted toward the area where Jack had been standing.

Catwoman swiveled her head then reverted her attention to Leo. "Name."

"What?"

She placed a gloved hand on her hip, her index finger tapping. "Of the Draco Malfoy who set this up."

She'd scored some serious points for recognizing the character. "Jackson Frost the Third."

"Never heard of him."

Why would she have? "Consider yourself lucky."

Her lips pursed, she stared down at him for a long moment. Then she muttered, "What the hell," and dropped her very attractive behind onto the opposite seat. "So, this is your idea of an easy place to pick up chicks in costume?"

Not only was the question out of place, it bore an uncanny similarity to something he might have said to his cat. "Well...one in particular, I guess. What's your name, by the way?"

"Cat."

She had to be joking. Or she obfuscated on purpose. He decided on the latter. After all, keeping one's identity hidden made for a great exit strategy. "Mine's Leo."

She lifted the leather menu and opened it, blocking his view of her face. "I know."

Madame Eve must employ a double standard, revealing the identity of men and not women. Another possible theory was Jack had forged the card and kept the woman's details a secret on purpose. Both explanations seemed plausible. "What else do you know about me?"

She flipped a page. "Everything."

Talk about unfair. Catwoman must have received an actual profile, complete with a photo and an option to decline the date. "It might not be all true."

She tilted the menu forward an inch, revealing the top half of her masked face. "What?"

"The profile you read. Jack has a weird sense of humor. You shouldn't trust any of it."

Her eyelids lowered into a slight squint, something the non-human Cat he knew had a habit of doing whenever he forgot to grab his keys. "I don't follow."

"It's obvious you received some basic information about me." When she shook her head, he waved off the denial. "It's not a big deal, but I thought I should tell you someone else filled everything out. Since I hadn't been offered a file on you at all, we should pretend this is a normal date and start over."

With a shrug and a swift nod, she put the menu down, pulled her gloves off, and reached an arm across the table. The smile she sent him made his stomach do an unsettling flip. "My name is Catalina Gato. I'm a maid, accountant, and shape-shifting witch with a clueless boss and very meddlesome sister."

What a sense of humor. Considering her costume, cat burglar would have been funnier, but she deserved bonus points for saying it all with a straight face. He took her hand and fought the odd urge to grab her, kiss her silly, and tear her clothes off.

The candle's flame changed from blue to white. Then the fire shot up in a straight line, six inches high. Another round of nervous clapping followed.

Their palms still touching, he frowned. "Someone here must love Halloween. These special effects are over the top, not to mention dangerous."

She shook her head and broke contact. Hints of disbelief and resignation laced her bell-like laugh. "Do you think Gomez has recovered enough to send a waiter our way?"

Taking a sip of chardonnay, Cat moved pieces of seared salmon around with her fork. Despite clearly making most of its profits from alcohol sales, The Cigar Lounge had an excellent chef. Too bad frayed nerves, the constraining bodysuit, and sexual frustration limited her appetite.

She was on a date with her boss. She'd fantasized about a moment like this, but the actual experience left her imagination in the dust. Since she'd watched Leo put on the outfit earlier, his appearance tonight shouldn't have made much of an impact. After all, she'd chosen his shoes and even timed his cufflink-selection process out of sheer boredom.

But something about the way his skin glowed under white candlelight changed her perspective. Gone was the clean-shaven, Clorox-wielding neat freak, the dorky *Supernatural*-obsessed couch potato. In his place sat a black-suit wearing man with a dark five o'clock shadow, an aura of mystery, and a flair for magic. Combined with his white Phantom mask, the possessive gleam in those sapphire eyes lent her warlock a dangerous edge.

His gaze lingered over her breasts. One corner of his mouth lifted. Since modern fashion made larger cup sizes a shopping nightmare, his undisguised appreciation did wonders for her body image. Remembering how his desire had manifested in a column of fire, she shivered. Such lack of control might warn most witches away, but she found his raw power exhilarating.

Sensing the attraction went both ways worsened her position. Currents of masculine possession rolled off him in waves, the molten psychic energy making her heart pound. He'd never learned to put up filters or shields, and their bond served as a conduit for his darkest fantasies.

As he undressed her with his gaze, she could almost feel her back zipper sliding down, his fingers tracing her spine to splay over her lower back. Her body responded with damp heat. She closed her eyes and saw him bend her over the table, his hands squeezing her breasts as he positioned himself behind her. When she lifted her lids to stare at his face, the intensity of his expression made her squirm. Color tinged his cheeks. He breathed shallow and fast. Though uncertain who'd initiated it, she had no doubt they'd shared the vision.

Remembering the consequences of letting their lust take its natural course, she tried to sever the connection. Her body trembling, she focused on physical sensations—the cold metal pressing into her palm, the smooth tablecloth under her free hand. The once crystal-clear image shimmered into a blurred overlay, but she could feel him spreading her, the rough pads of his fingers burning a path up her shaking thighs. Cool air washed over her sweat-slicked face, chilling the back of her neck where his warm breath lingered. A shaft of heat speared between her legs, forcing her to bite her lower lip to stem a cry. Using the pain, she wrenched herself out of the fantasy.

Catching her breath, she observed his dazed expression. He had no idea of what he'd done. Staying here, playing this game with him, was too dangerous. The moment she'd realized who her one-night stand was, she should have left. A warlock-familiar bond was intimate enough without complicating the situation with sex.

Though she couldn't read his thoughts word for word, she had constant access to his mind. To channel his power, her abilities allowed her to sense his needs and desires. The connection worked both ways, which was why they achieved more than the bare minimum communication even when she took animal form. It also amplified the potential psychic effect of anything they both wanted. Right now, it happened to be sex.

This level of intimacy complicated matters. While Wiccan norms didn't flat out forbid fraternization between master and minion, such affairs tended to end in one of two ways. Either all hell broke loose when the pair split, the ensuing melodramatic supernatural shit storm creating a spectacle worthy of any reality show, or the relationship progressed at light speed toward promises of *Till death do us part*. Option one came with too much craziness, and option two required too much commitment. Though she liked and lusted after the warlock, she had no intention of settling down at twenty-three. On the cusp of regaining the freedom to travel the world upon her contract's termination, she didn't want to be tied to anyone but herself.

This one-night stand needed to end here. It should have never started. She chalked up her moment of weakness to not having eaten a decent dinner in six months. Confinement gave her a new appreciation for good food and ambiance, and having it already paid for came as a huge plus. It had nothing to do with the fantasy she'd like to cling to for a little longer—the game of make-believe where they were two unattached strangers who could walk out together and do as they pleased. "Why do you keep staring at me?"

Having made a huge dent in his massive Bistecca Fiorentina, Leo nursed a glass of Pinot Noir while watching her with undisguised fascination. "Something about you is oddly familiar."

She focused on assembling perfect bites: a morsel of salmon, a bit of tomato, topped with a drizzle of sauce. Nothing about fish could be construed as sexual. "We're both wearing masks."

"It must be the eyes. I've seen them before." He carved a sizable chunk of red meat and forked it over to her plate.

He could say that again. She cut a small piece of steak and tried it. Though rarer than she preferred, it appealed to all her taste buds. "The food here is great," she mumbled, reminding herself to focus on innocuous first-date conversation and not vivid fantasies of public sex.

He took the hint and stole a corner of her salmon. "So, tell me, who's your favorite Batman?"

"George Clooney," she replied with a straight face.

His fork paused in the air. "And here I thought we might

have had something."

Laughter bubbled. When her attempt to subdue it almost resulted in suffocation, she raised her hand to cover her mouth. Her shoulders shaking, she asked, "Let me guess. You prefer your Batmen dark and broody."

He shook his head. "Chicks seem to fall for the suave smile and twinkling brown eyes, acting ability be damned."

Her nose twitched. "On behalf of my entire gender, I accept your apology. As for the eyes, I'm partial to blue."

He tilted his head forward. "Are you now? By the way, you're wasting all this food."

Watching him chew and swallow her salmon with gusto, she sighed. "In all honesty, it's hard to breathe in this outfit, let alone expand my tummy."

Why did the man's grin have to make her stomach flutter? Not jumping his bones was a difficult enough decision without him upping the temptation factor.

"I always tell people vanity is never worth discomfort, but in your case, I'd be lying."

Giving up on the meal, she set her fork down. "Says someone who wears the male accessory trifecta—tie clip, cufflinks, and luxury watch."

He took another bite of her fish. "You'll notice none of these affect my ability to eat."

Good point. "Being a man must be nice."

"Can you imagine wearing a suit five days a week and never being able to deviate from dark business colors?" he asked with a crooked grin, the feigned sufferance in his tone so exaggerated, she had to laugh. "There aren't many shades of black and blue to choose from."

She placed one elbow on the table and rested her chin on her palm. In a grave voice, she attempted commiseration. "How do you manage to cope?"

He wiggled his eyebrows. "Lots of colorful socks."

She'd always wondered why he owned such an expansive collection. "What's the point, if no one sees them?"

He took a long swill of wine. "Why do women buy fancy underwear?"

Touché. She placed her free hand on the table and drew circles with her thumbnail. "In case someone takes our clothes off."

His gaze drifted once more to her chest area. "By then, a guy's focus won't be on the lingerie, no matter how expensive."

Remembering the circumstances behind this date, her face burned. Considering she needed to cut the night short, she should quit flirting. But the words flowed with such ease she couldn't bring herself to stop. "You'll be disappointed. There was no way I could squeeze into this cat suit without a sports bra."

He didn't miss a beat. "I find exercise outfits very sexy."

She resisted the urge to fidget. "In all fairness, I need to tell you...."

"We're not having sex tonight? I realized it ten minutes into dinner."

She blinked. "Oh?"

He reached over and patted the back of her hand. "Someone who reads every single page on a menu isn't going to jump into bed with a man on a first date. I get it. But if we go on a second date, tomorrow, the label no longer applies. While we're on the subject, what are your plans for the rest of this weekend?"

Snuggling on his lap while watching a *Warehouse 13* marathon, an awesome activity if she didn't have to be in cat form. "I like you, I really do. But I—"

"You have a boyfriend."

She shook her head. "Of course not. I wouldn't be here, if I did."

"You're about to leave the city for an extended period."

She wished. "Nope. Pretty much stuck here for the foreseeable future."

"You're suffering from a debilitating or fatal illness."

She wrinkled her nose. "You're reaching, counselor."

"I'm not the courtroom kind of lawyer." He leaned back in his chair and played with the stem of his wine glass. "You find

41

me attractive, so it can't be the problem."

He was right, but it seemed appropriate to play coy. "You sound pretty sure of yourself."

He grinned. "Your whole face turns pink when you blush. And I can tell when a woman wants to do bad things to me."

So, Mr. Dork had a naughty side. The man was smooth—a little too smooth. "Fine. You're hot. But...."

He had the audacity to nod. "I work hard for this physique. Hours upon hours of sweat, blood, and tears, all for your viewing pleasure. I also don't have a criminal record, do make a decent salary, and should have convinced you I'm not a psycho by now. I deserve your contact info, at the very least."

And she would have given it to him, but it happened to be his home phone. Since she never left the house, communicating via the Internet had made more sense than buying a mobile device. "Here's the thing—"

He leaned forward. "You can always reject my calls if you later decide I'm crazy."

She scowled. "Will you let me finish?"

He sent her a mock salute. "Yes ma'am." He straightened in his chair, enhancing the effect. How was she supposed to extricate herself if he kept making her giggle like a schoolgirl?

She switched tactics. Maybe she could convince him he didn't want another date. "Why are you asking to see me again anyway? We're still strangers, for all intents and purposes."

His chin lifted, his face forming an expression of affront. "I beg to differ. I've gathered a ton of important details. We *have* spent over an hour together, and you're very chatty."

She lifted an eyebrow in challenge. "Oh, yeah? What about me makes you want my number?"

Placing his elbows on the table, he steepled his fingers. "You're close to your family, even the little sister you complained about. Since I'm a bit of a mama's boy, it gives us something in common."

The man *did* call his parents on a weekly basis. "For most girls, being close to your mother is not a selling point."

He rolled his eyes. "I don't see why not. After all, someone else has already trained me well and eliminated a bunch of nasty male habits."

She had to concede this round. He never made a mess and cooked halfway-decent breakfasts. "So far, you've described one of my traits, and it applies to at least half the world's female population. Any other reason for this sudden attraction?"

He nodded, his expression grave. "You laughed at all my *Star Trek* jokes, identified which show 'frack' came from, and admitted your crush on Dean Winchester. By the way, isn't he a little short for you?"

She'd smiled so much since her arrival, her face muscles had grown fatigued. "Nope. I looked it up. Jensen Ackles is six foot one, which means he has three inches on me. You, Mr. Smarty-pants, have two, at the most."

He narrowed his eyes. "Two and a half. By the way, if you could wear flats on our next outing, I'd appreciate it. It'd go well with a nice summer dress."

She'd never realized he could be so persistent. "You're giving me fashion advice now?"

"You admitted your sister bought this costume, which means I've yet to ascertain your clothing tastes. By the way, I'm good at holding bags while women shop. My mother told me I had a talent for it back when I was eight. I'll even help you throw away the packaging when you get home."

Remembering how maniacal he was about immediate disposal of rubbish, she couldn't hold back a belly chuckle. "You're assuming I'll come home with you."

"Imagine a soft leather couch in front of a 60-inch flat screen, showing your choice of entertainment, even if it's *Grey's Anatomy*. A bucket of stovetop popcorn drizzled with smoked sea salt and olive oil, along with a tall frosty glass of Diet Coke. Given appropriate incentive, I might even massage your tired feet." Temptation laced his voice, the allure almost supernatural. He shouldn't command any non-elemental powers, but her overwhelming desire to say yes made her suspicious.

43

Shaking her head for a return to clarity, she managed a half-hearted snort. "I'm not that naive. I can tell you're a remote-hogger."

He seemed to give the accusation some thought. "Okay, maybe not a Patrick Dempsey show. The rest of the scenario, I can deliver."

If only she could take him up on it. "Why do you want to do this with me? I'm sure you can find other girls with television addictions."

He cleared his throat. "I'm not sure if anyone's told you this, but you're drop-dead gorgeous."

As a matter of fact, no one had ever used those words to describe her. How was any woman supposed to resist such blatant masculine appreciation? "Black is a slimming color. I look worse with my clothes off."

"I doubt it." His gaze wobbled, but he managed to maintain eye contact. "It's too early in our relationship for me to make specific counterarguments, but I can't wait for the time when I'll have the necessary visual data to support my theory."

She sighed. "You're like a dog with a bone."

"Since you'd be the bone, I won't take offense." In a move so quick, she saw only a blur, he grabbed her hand. The moment he made skin contact, the candle's white flame rose by a few inches again. He didn't seem to notice he'd used magic twice in less than two seconds. He brought her fingers to his lips. "So, how's my case, so far?"

Her resolve wavered. She couldn't give him the fairy tale, but what was the harm in sex? Once the idea presented itself, the delicious possibilities took hold and spread to obliterate all caution. This was All Hallows' Eve, her single night off. After the six months she'd been through and the eighteen to come, she deserved to throw caution to the wind and act as she pleased. "No dice on the phone number, but...."

"But?" A half-grin belied his confidence.

"But you were wrong about me not seeing this one-night stand through."

Chapter Four

"You brought an overnight bag?" Leo asked as they walked away from the reception desk. He'd always thought he had a gift for reading people, but Cat kept him off-balance. They'd met before, he'd bet his life on it. But the when, where, and how continued to elude him.

She stuffed her gloves into the mid-sized duffel they'd retrieved from the front desk. Dimples formed in her cheeks when she faced him and smiled. "I came prepared to stay the night." When he stared at her, she nodded. "Doing the walk of shame in an all-leather Catwoman costume would be a new low, not to mention uncomfortable."

He glanced at the pink satchel, his brain working overtime to tease apart the anomaly. Then he matched its length with the height of her boots. "You changed into the costume here, didn't you? It's why you have spare clothes."

She tripped on her own feet, but he'd been prepared to catch her. Very few things pleased him more than being right. Closing his hands around her waist, he pulled her in to his chest and filled his lungs with her scent. She smelled fresh and minty.

"I'll take that as a yes. Any chance you'll let me carry the bag for you?"

She softened in his arms for a moment before her spine snapped straight. "I don't need a man to lift my stuff. You think you're very smart, don't you?"

"It's a proven fact." His parents had his IQ tested at the age of five, after sending him to an expensive kindergarten for future geniuses. His scoring a few points shy of the categorization had been a huge disappointment, or so he'd been told.

Reaching the small bank of elevators, she pressed the up button. "But you didn't expect me to sleep with you tonight."

He leaned his shoulder against the cold marble. She had such a superior expression, he couldn't resist commenting. "I'm pretty sure you didn't plan on coming up until about fifteen minutes ago."

She shrugged. "I'll admit it. This was a spur-of-the-moment decision. But once I set my mind to something, I see it through—despite the possibility of dire consequences."

Why had it taken him this long to realize he appreciated honesty in women? "If you end up backpedaling, I like to think I'd be cool with it."

"You're not sure?" She slung the thick strap over one shoulder. Contrasting black and shocking pink made for a comical combination.

"Let's just say, I'd use every trick in the book to get you to change your mind." And thanks to Jack and their colorful past, he had a number of ideas at his disposal.

Thick metal doors slid open. They marched into the empty elevator. An older model, it had a bronze front, mirrors on the three walls, and beige marble floors. He sniffed the air and smiled at the scent of disinfectant and polish.

As the exit sealed shut, she pivoted to face him. "So, what do you plan on doing to me in the No Dreams Required suite?"

The old-school dial edged along the semicircle of numbers to indicate their ascent. He caught her chin and circled her waist with his other arm. "Naughty things."

Her eyes widened. She lifted one hand to rest on his chest. In her high heels, she stood an inch taller than him, so he tipped her head back for better access. Her mouth opened in an invitation to kiss, but he chose first to nibble the luscious lower lip that had taunted him for the past hour and half. Drawing the soft, plump flesh into his mouth, he teased it not too gently with his teeth.

Delicate fingers laced through his hair. Blunt nails dug into his scalp. With a moan, she mirrored his caress and slid her other hand up to rest against his neck. The trembling tips of her fingers, the sinuous arch of her back—each subtle sign of surrender sent his pulse racing and spread liquid heat over his skin. Consumed by the possessive instinct to devour, he pushed his tongue into her mouth, tangling it with hers.

Her duffel's strap slid down to hang over the crook of her elbow. Making a frustrated sound in her throat, she unfolded her arm and let the bag drop to the floor. Wobbling, she clutched his lapel and stepped back, pulling him with her.

He plastered her against the side of the elevator. She whimpered, and his hazed brain interpreted the muted sound as both permission and a demand for more. He wedged his knee between her legs, closed his hand over her breast. When he relinquished her mouth to kiss a path down her neck, she tilted her head to the side, her soft cries fueling his fiery hunger as her hair tickled his cheek. Her hips shifting forward and back, she rode his thigh as he sucked red marks over her golden skin.

The elevator chimed, announcing their imminent arrival at the designated floor. Straightening, he struggled to fill his lungs, satisfied to see her in no better condition. Her chest heaving, she rested the back of her head against the mirrored wall. Needing to see more than her kiss-swollen lips, he yanked off her mask. Her flushed, rounded cheeks were the color of coral, her half-closed lids rimmed with long, dark lashes. The vulnerability reflected on her exquisite face sent his arousal into overdrive. A primitive male instinct told him he could have her here and now.

A loud crack accompanied the elevator's lurch to a complete stop. The incandescent lights above their heads flashed before blowing out in a burst of sparks. He launched forward, tucking her body into his chest. A breath later, they were in complete darkness.

"*Hijo de puta.*" She sounded more annoyed than scared. "I had a feeling something like this might happen."

He'd expected a strong reaction, but this one didn't quite fit. She wriggled in his hold. "I need to see. Where's your phone?"

Impressed and a little suspicious of her calm, he reached into his breast pocket and pulled out his BlackBerry. Pressing a key at random, he turned the screen on. Before he could say a word, she grabbed it, shoved him off her, and held the phone against the elevator's keypad. A moment later, she jammed her finger onto the emergency call button.

Nothing happened.

Muttering a stream of incomprehensible, angry-sounding words, she slapped the BlackBerry into his palm. "Unlock it."

She seemed to speak in shorter sentences when angry. "I'm sure someone will—"

"Call the front desk. Now," she growled.

Thanking his lucky stars for CDMA networks, which gave him the single but life-saving bar of reception in the elevator, he pulled up his call history and redialed the number he'd used to confirm his dinner reservation. After several rings, Gomez's voice crackled over the earpiece. "The Cigar Lounge."

"Hi. This is Leo Difuoco. I'm stuck in the elevator. Can you put me in touch with someone in charge?"

The man complied with commendable swiftness. Not long after, he was speaking with a woman who identified herself as the client relations manager. Massaging the bridge of his nose, he fought the urge to cut off her slew of equivocations and excuses, the length of which boded ill. "I regret to inform you, Mr. Difuoco, but the elevator car is stuck between two floors and the doors face a concrete wall. It's an older model, so there's no escape hatch on the ceiling."

He cast a furtive glance in the direction of the dark shadow he could barely make out as his date. He heard a rhythmic tapping sound he guessed came from fingers drumming on the wall. "So, what's the good news?"

"The good news is you're secure where you are. We've called

in an engineering team to address the problem. The process might take a few hours, but since this elevator model isn't airtight, there's no risk of suffocation."

Aside from a woman who seemed on the verge of strangling him. "I see. Is there any way you can activate the emergency lights?"

"Again, I apologize. We aren't certain what caused the surge of electricity that shorted the circuits, and we don't want to risk doing more damage. Please hang tight; help is on its why. I also suggest you get off the phone to conserve battery life in case we need to contact you later."

Murmuring a thank you, he hung up. "So...."

"I heard. There's nothing they can do, so we're stuck here for a few hours."

He added cat-like hearing to her list of odd quirks. "I can keep the screen lit—"

"Shh.... I'm thinking."

There were times when a man needed to keep his mouth shut. He couldn't fathom why, but he had a sneaking suspicion she blamed him for what had transpired, which was rather unfair. He waited. And waited. And waited some more. "Umm.... So, are you—?"

She snapped her fingers. An instant later, four floating globes of light appeared above them, bathing the elevator in a soft yellow glow. Dropping the phone, he lurched back, the momentum sending his head crashing into the opposite wall. "What the fuck?"

She placed her hands on her hips. "I wasn't about to stay here in the dark when a little spell would solve the problem."

Magic, yeah, right. "Very funny. You've had your laugh. So, where are the cameras?"

Her jaw dropped. "You must be shitting me. After all this, you're still in denial?"

He pivoted to his right and banged at the elevator door. "Okay, guys. I don't care what Jack Frost told you, but I didn't sign up for a reality TV show. I'm a lawyer, and I will sue your ass into bankruptcy if you don't let me out right this instant."

"Urghh...." Her heels crashed on the floor, broadcasting her stomping advance. Small but surprisingly strong hands grabbed his shoulder, swung him around, and shoved him against the door. "Listen to me." Her fingers and thumb dug into his cheeks. "This might not be the best way to break this to you, but I've had it. I'm hot, sweaty, and stuck in an elevator on my damn night off." Her other hand lifted to rest on her hips. "You're a warlock. You come from a bloodline with uber-powerful fire mages, and your inability to control your power broke this elevator."

He raised an eyebrow and nodded. "Uh-huh. Sure. Has anyone told you you're a great actress? Whoa, there—" Her stiletto hovered an inch away from the top of his Italian leather shoes. "Those are expensive."

Her jaw muscles ticked. Then she narrowed her green eyes and disappeared with a soft popping sound. Okay, he had to admit—the stunt she'd pulled off impressed him.

He scrutinized the ceiling, searching for wires and a hatch.

"Meow."

He froze. A moment later, a black cat, *his* cat, stared up at him with Catalina's emerald eyes.

White flames appeared out of nowhere, heading straight for the feline. With a loud hiss, the cat jumped into his arms. Catching her, he spun, blocking the danger with his back. Squeezing her tight, he braced for impact. He didn't care what was going on, but no way was he letting her get hurt.

When none of his clothing went up in smoke, he twisted his neck to glance over his shoulder. The balls of blazing fire hovered in place, forming an arc around his body.

With another popping sound, something soft and warm pushed his arms apart. Before his disbelieving eyes, the furry creature morphed into a curvy feminine frame. Once again, he stared into deep-green eyes, but this time, they were housed in a human face.

Stress lines bracketing her mouth, Cat rested one hand against his cheek. "Leo. You need to calm down. Your flames are real. They can burn me."

Either he'd sustained some sort of head trauma when the elevator stalled, resulting in vivid hallucinations, or there might be some truth to her *Twilight Zone* supposition. How could she think he'd ever attack her with fireballs? "They're not mine, I swear. I'd never hurt you."

She nodded. "I believe you. It's why I took a chance. Your subconscious created them—it's been burning away every attempt I've made to show you the truth. Please, listen. Concentrate on the flames and pull the power back inside you."

She sounded so certain. If she was telling the truth, he was officially an asshole of epic proportions. "I'm not sure...."

"Look into my eyes, focus on what you want, and visualize the energy seeping away. Those fires are your creation, so fixing this should be a piece of cake."

Certain he'd gone insane, he maintained eye contact with her and imagined the flames shrinking. He couldn't see the result, but the interior's brightness decreased by several orders of magnitude. "Okay, this is one fucked-up dream."

She responded with an impatient snort, but the corners of her lips curved up as she peeked over his shoulder. "Did I say weaken the fires? No, I said take them out. Connect with them. They're part of you. They'll do whatever you want. You can handle this."

Her encouraging smile and hopeful expression made it impossible not to embrace the madness. He twisted his neck around so he could glare at the offensive white targets. He could almost see clear blurring waves forming a direct link between him and the flames. Following her earlier direction, he drew a breath and tried to visualize the molecules of energy flowing into his body. As the fires dimmed and went out, he experienced a surge of power. His fingertips tingled, and it felt as if he were floating in thin air.

Which made sense, since he'd somehow lifted them both a foot off the floor. "Gah...."

She laughed, pulled off the mask he'd forgotten he was

wearing, and smacked a closed-mouthed kiss on his cheek.

"Focus, young grasshopper. We'll explore levitation when you get over your control issues." She pointed at the floor. "Put me down."

Easier said than done. "Mind talking me through this trick?"

Tossing the mask aside, she shook her head. "It needs to come naturally. You're a powerful warlock. If you don't want to float, you won't. Take charge."

He cleared his throat. "If you haven't noticed, I'm not a take-charge kind of guy."

She rolled her eyes. "Of course, you are. You ordered dinner for me."

"I made a suggestion, and I did it after you spent fifteen minutes contemplating the meaning of food as we know it."

Resting her arms on his shoulders, she canted her head. "You bamboozled me into coming up to your hotel room with you."

He frowned. "I remember a very different sequence of events."

"Leo." He loved the emerald twinkle in her eye.

"Yes." He rubbed the tip of his nose over hers.

"You can let me go."

Only now did he realize they once again stood on solid ground. "Do I have to?"

"Sorry, but yes."

"Why?"

She wrinkled her nose. "I'm overheating. I get cranky when I overheat. Your fire stunt raised the temperature in here by several degrees. All I want to do right now is get naked."

The idea sent blood pooling straight to his penis. With much reluctance, he unlaced his fingers. It boggled the mind how he could be aroused again after all this excitement. Then a horrible thought occurred to him. "Did you create an illusion to appear as my cat, or are you my cat?"

Sitting on the marble floor, she unzipped her left boot and yanked it off. "I'm your familiar." She repeated the process on her right leg.

"If you wouldn't mind defining the term...?"

Cat wore the cutest pink booty socks. She pulled them off, balled them up, and tossed them in the general direction of her footwear. Neatness didn't seem to be one of her virtues, but he could learn to live with it.

"I'm a non-elemental *human* witch who signed an apprenticeship contract with your great-aunt. When she died, the remainder of my contract term passed on to you."

He scratched his head. "I hate to tell you this, but you made a crap employment deal. You never want to be stuck with a boss you haven't met. Why did you stay a cat all this time?"

Cheeks puffed and nose scrunched, she sprang into a standing position. Getting rid of her boots wouldn't have cooled her down much since the leather suit reached all the way to her ankles. "There's a clause preventing me from showing my human form in your vicinity or leaving your house without your express permission. Aren't you hot?"

Come to think of it, he was sweating buckets. He took off his tie clip and cufflinks and placed them in the breast pocket not already holding his wallet. Then he shrugged off his suit jacket and laid it on top of her duffel. "Sounds like one fucked-up arrangement. Why would anyone sign such a thing?"

She helped him undo his tie, which felt like a noose around his neck in the heat. "Those terms are almost never enforced. The language in the boilerplate Familiar Employment Agreement has been passed down over the centuries, so it's a bit outdated. Almost every witch or warlock waives those two clauses straight away. Nonna did it when she hired me, but you needed to repeat the ritual after the rights transferred. You didn't."

He yanked the silk free, folded it, and dropped it on top of his jacket. "I'm new at this whole warlock thing, but someone should consider rewriting the document. This explains a lot, though. So, when I came home to find my cat soaking wet a few months back...."

Unbuttoning his top three buttons, she nodded. "I was

taking a shower. You came within ten feet of me, and I shifted into a cat. I can't control it."

To think he could have had a hot, occasionally naked chick in his house this entire time instead of a cranky feline. He folded his cuffs to under his elbows. "So, what changed today?"

She lifted her index finger. "I get one night off. All Hallows' Eve."

Whoever had first drafted this contract needed to be burned at the stake.

She crouched and began to untie his laces, prompting him to yelp and follow her down. "Let me do it."

Once done, he carried his shoes and socks to the far corner of the elevator. Unable to shut his neat freak down, he reached for her boots.

She stood up, shook her head, and lifted her gaze to the ceiling. Without warning, all the loose items in the elevator levitated. Her socks rolled themselves into a little ball and slid into her duffel's side pouch, along with both their masks. The bag somehow unzipped itself, and a pair of flat sandals flew out, settling on the floor near his shoes. Folded dark denim, a T-shirt, pink bra and panties, and a rather large cosmetics bag lifted into the air, remaining there as her boots slid into the duffel. Re-zipping itself, the satchel landed next to their footwear, her change of clothes floating down on top. His suit jacket and tie soon followed. She topped off the pile with his BlackBerry.

Certain he hadn't performed magic in the past ten seconds, something clicked. "I *have* heard your voice before. You're the maid." After a moment's thought, he added, "You're also Nonna's—I mean, my accountant. Why didn't you say something over the phone?"

She pointed up. "I conjured four illumination globes, which is a high-level illusion spell, by the way, and you reacted by searching for a camera."

In his defense, it was what any sane person would have done in his shoes. "So, you used your holiday to track me down?"

"Of course not. I decided to get laid. I planned on riding out my last eighteen months of service after having some no-strings-attached sex."

He had no idea why the revelation irritated him. "You should have at least given telling me the truth a shot."

She marched forward until they stood toe-to-toe. "I have some sense of self-preservation. All of my notes to you went up in smoke, my e-mail made your computer go bye-bye, and you almost barbecued me five minutes ago. Oh, your eyes are now green instead of blue, which is kind of creepy. Please tell me you're not jealous of yourself."

He stared at his reflection in the mirror. It took a few blinks and some concentration to make the almost-fluorescent color go away. "Point taken. And, of course, I'm not jealous," he lied. Her wanting to sleep with anyone else after living with him for six months irked him to an absurd degree.

"Very convincing." Her tone gave a whole new meaning to the word facetious.

He decided to change the topic. Maintaining eye contact, he tried to imbue his voice with the utmost sincerity. "You have no idea how sorry I am for the—umm—spontaneous combustion incidents. Let's get this out of the way. You're a free woman—cat—familiar—whatever. You can come and go as you please, and you don't need to be a cat in front of me ever again."

She tapped his temple with her index finger. "Do you seriously think it's that easy?"

He had, yes. "Is there something more elaborate I need to do?"

She crossed her arms and looked him up and down as if he were daft, which, from her point of view, made some sense. "You need to get the contract from the safe in the basement, sign it in blood to take ownership of me then read out the incantation as written in the document."

He furrowed his brows. "What basement?"

Her mouth twitched from side to side, reminding him of her cat form. All she needed were whiskers. "The door is under the first floor staircase. It's warded to appear as a concrete wall."

"Of course it is. And this safe...?"

"You'll see it as a standard-issue cauldron. I'll lead you to it when we get home. Any other questions?"

He had a nagging suspicion he'd donated several very dangerous items to the Salvation Army. Maybe he had time to buy them back. It wasn't like a crescent headboard, blood-red carpet, and gargantuan mirror would have flown off the shelves. And how dangerous could magic candles be? "Why in holy hell would anyone want to have or be a familiar?"

She pointed at the pile of stuff stacked in one corner. "With my powers alone, all this telekinesis would have drained me, making any further tricks out of the question for days." With her index finger, she drew a circle in the small space between them. "But you leak so much power, I can do this," she snapped her fingers, "and teleport these from my bag without even thinking twice."

She handed him one of the two wet wipes before cleaning her own face and hands. Once he'd followed suit, she grabbed his and placed both in the center of her palm, holding it between them. "You might be the source of all my juice, but you can't do any of the things I did. All you have is raw elemental power. You can manipulate energy molecules to lift stuff off the ground, which more or less sums up your repertoire of useful spells. You can, however, make this trash go up in smoke. Go ahead. Try it."

He cast an uneasy glance at her hand. "Shouldn't you put those someplace safe?"

Her cheeky smile was equal parts unnerving and encouraging. "Your magic was going haywire because you rejected it. We've solved the problem. Now, think about a cold fire, with a low burning point, and focus on not hurting me."

With a sigh, he gave it a try. To his surprise, green flames consumed the wipes less than a second later without creating any smoke or doing damage to the person holding them. Now, *that* was cool.

Before he was done patting himself on the back, she smiled and spun on her heel. "Since we've established your newfound control, help me take this damn suit off."

Chapter Five

*L*eo froze. Instinct told him where this was heading, but due to the odd location, he'd rather have verbal confirmation. "You want me to take your clothes off?"

She tapped one bare foot on the marble floor. "Pull the zipper down, please. I'm going to pass out from heat exhaustion any moment now."

Talk about ambiguous. "So, this is for comfort purposes?"

"Don't be so jumpy. I'm changing into something more relaxed. I've seen you in the shower plenty of times."

The reminder she'd seen him naked, *watched* him undress, and slept next to him messed with his head. Intense attraction and uncomfortable erection aside, the logical course of action was to take a step back and slow things down. He hadn't quite figured out the whole warlock-familiar business yet, and he didn't think it wise to complicate matters right this instant. Of course, the possibility of sex in an elevator with her would make him take the risk in two seconds flat. "I want to make something clear. *You* stripping in front of me here will have serious repercussions."

She tapped the side of her neck, her fingers pointing to the suit's collar. "You're being paranoid. If there were surveillance cameras in here, you'd have fried them along with the rest of the electronics."

He hadn't even thought about the possibility of being videoed. "It's not what I meant. As we've learned, my self-control is on the iffy side. I should tell you—"

"You burned away something on my palm without hurting me. It'll be fine. I can't stay in this thing for two more minutes, let alone hours. I don't see what the big deal is. I'm wearing a sports bra and cycling shorts."

"Oh." He must have misinterpreted the entire situation. Talk about setting a sexually frustrated guy up for a huge letdown. "You should have led with that."

She grunted. "I told you about it at dinner."

As he yanked the tab down, the metal hinges came apart with a soft whirring sound. "I can't be expected to remember a conversation from hours ago."

The zipper seemed to go on for miles, ending halfway down her butt. The leather separated to reveal a lower back with enough flesh to give a smooth finish to what appeared to be solid muscle. His gaze followed her spine to the flimsy black lace circling her hips.

His jaw dropped. "You're wearing a thong."

"You know your female undergarments."

As far as unmistakable invitations went, this fit the bill. "You said you were wearing shorts."

"I lied." She faced him. Pulling her arms free of the sleeves, she pushed the suit down to her waist. "What?"

Plain black sports bra or no, he couldn't peel his gaze from her luscious breasts. His mouth went dry. As they were, they'd overflow his hands. How big would they be without the flattening undergarment?

Kneeling, he hooked his fingers under the leather. "Let me help you take this off."

Cat released a pent-up breath as Leo pulled the leather suit down to her ankles. Thank goodness he'd taken the hint. How could any man be so dense? Any more obvious, and she'd be flashing a bright neon sign saying *get me naked*.

And while recent revelations might be exciting and life-changing news to him, for her they were mundane. The last thing she wanted to do was spend the next two hours yapping about boring energy dynamics, contracts, or employment terms. She had a much better idea for wiling away the time.

With him so close and no longer fighting their connection, her body buzzed with excess energy. She could use it to move the elevator up a few feet, open the doors, and leave, but why waste a golden opportunity?

She'd always fantasized about having sex in a quasi-public place. Modern-day surveillance technology stripped most avenues of viability, but her warlock's little power explosion had taken care of the biggest hurdle. Once she'd confirmed his full control over magic and subsequently decreased the risk of accidental combustion, the single remaining barrier was the psychic link turned possible melodrama or potential soul mate conundrum. After pondering the associated downsides for about ten seconds, she decided to deal with the repercussions later. Some opportunities were meant to be grabbed, kissed, and tempted into doing kinky things.

She stepped out of her suit and teleported it into her duffel. If the man had dilly-dallied for much longer, she would have snapped her fingers and dematerialized the darn thing from her body, potential disaster from lack of experience be damned. She kind of wished she'd done it on the off chance he'd have fainted from shock.

Then again, if she'd rendered him unconscious, she wouldn't have been able to witness the stunned, worshipful expression he wore right now. "Like what you see?"

"You have very nice legs."

She was rather partial to them herself. Keeping her limbs toned had always been a piece of cake. Her boobs and butt were another story.

He closed his fingers around the backs of her knees, pressed his lips against her inner thigh, and nibbled. "I warned you about serious repercussions."

She had to give it to the warlock. Once his head was in the game, he seemed capable of some creative moves.

Batting her eyelashes, she laced her fingers through his dark curls. The strands flowed like silk over her skin. "I'm *sooo* scared."

He bit her, hard enough to elicit a yelp. "Doesn't this damn contract have a clause about respect?"

"It's my night off, for me to do with as I please."

He blew a hot breath over the mark he'd left, making it nearly impossible to stay upright. "And what do you want?"

It took every ounce of self-control to maintain a half-joking tone. "I was promised multiple orgasms."

He kissed another patch of skin, higher up on her leg, this time. "I doubt Madame Eve would be so crude." His tongue lashed over the crease where her thigh and torso met. A shiver rolled down her spine, the sensation interfering with her balance even more. "But I think we can come up with a mutually acceptable arrangement."

Shifting to grip his shoulders, she braced her weight forward. "What can I give you?"

He slid his palms up to rest them on her bottom. "Complete obedience would be nice."

She clawed his deltoids. "I'll think about it."

He caught the scrap of lace between his teeth and pulled it to the side, causing heat to kindle between her legs. "Think fast."

She wondered when the power dynamic had shifted. "How about I let you take off my panties, for now?" If he didn't soon, she'd go insane.

An amused male chuckle preceded a sizzling sensation along the sides of her hips. Her thong drifted to the floor. Glancing down, she noticed singe marks on the fabric. "Show-off."

He met her gaze with a crooked grin. "You've heard the warning about playing with fire." Eyeing her bra, he cocked a brow. "You've been flirting with it all night."

And she was about to get burned—in the most delicious way possible. Deciding not to risk the more expensive undergarment, she reached one arm behind her and undid the clasp. A bout of shyness hit, and she clutched the separating straps, managing to hold them together in a shaky vise. While she might be at peace with most of her body, her breasts were a problem zone. The thought of exposing them made all her bravado go up in smoke.

"Allow me." Her breath caught as he stood. Why had she thought stripping in an enclosed space surrounded by mirrors would be a good idea? She'd been serious about looking better with clothes on.

Pulling her into his embrace, he grabbed her hand. With a truncated breath, she let go. A moment later, the pressure around her chest eased and the thick straps fell off her shoulders. She closed her eyes as the smooth material drifted down.

He cleared his throat. "I never pegged you as shy."

She snuck a peek and found herself in complete darkness. "Huh." She'd conjured the illumination globes, so it made sense they'd go away when she wanted to hide. Being a witch had its perks. "We don't need light, do we?"

Hearing soft footsteps and the rustle of clothing, she pivoted and tried to figure out where he'd gone. After a few aborted attempts to find him, hard muscle warmed her back, his short chest hair rough against her skin.

Hot breath grazed the sensitive spot behind her earlobe, making her toes curl. Strong fingers circled her waist. When he pushed her forward, she blindly reached out until she brushed a cool surface. The complete lack of texture made her guess a mirror rather than the brass doors. His larger body surrounded her, pressing into her until her elbows bent and her nipples grazed the wall. His trousers slid over the back of her legs, his belt buckle digging into her butt. Being seen made her feel vulnerable. Not seeing rendered her helpless.

His palms slid up her belly. She trembled, her breath catching when his thumb traced the side of her chest. Tortured by heightened awareness, she shifted to escape and found herself trapped. His mouth pressed against the back of her neck.

He sucked, his tongue pulsing over the spot and distracting her from his progress.

After what seemed like an eternity, he took possession of her aching breasts. She whimpered at the spine-tingling sensation when he cupped the heavy mounds. "I could play with these all day." He rolled one nipple between his thumb and forefinger, making her gasp at the duality of pleasure and pain.

Nudging her thighs apart, he slid his fingers along her torso, pushing down to trace the abdominal muscles hidden beneath her flesh. When he reached the apex of her legs, he used the heel of his palm to apply pressure over the already sensitive bundle of nerves. Parting her labia, he circled her wet opening. "I want to see you."

Panting, her arms dropped weakly to her sides. He traced her folds once more, teasing, touching, taunting, and never once pushing into her. She shifted her hips in search of relief. It felt as if static electricity coated her skin, making her hairs stand on end and her nerve endings go haywire wherever his arms and chest made contact. His zipper dug into her butt, reminding her of his growing arousal. She couldn't take much more.

"The lights, kitten."

With a surrendering moan, she used the last flickers of sanity to conjure a single yellow globe. She no longer cared what he thought, as long as he finished what he started. Her vision adjusted, her reflection coming into focus. She stared at it with disbelieving eyes, the naked apparition appearing as a stranger.

She'd lolled her head back, resting it against his shoulder. Her amber skin contrasted with his paler shade. Sweat plastered her short hair to the sides of her face. Her lips were blood red, her cheeks flushed. Lowered lids obscured her eyes beneath a curtain of lashes.

Her nipples had puckered into sharp points. A large male hand, covered in a light dusting of hair, enveloped her right breast. A muscled arm snaked down her torso, visually cutting her in half. Against the backdrop of his much larger body, her curves trapped within his almost predatory hold, she appeared vulnerable and distinctly feminine.

Blue eyes gleaming in the dim light, he brushed a kiss onto her temple. "Damn, you're beautiful."

She hadn't thought it possible, but her cheeks darkened to a more intense shade of coral. She met his reflection's gaze, her tongue wetting her parched lips. He shifted his head and bit her earlobe.

"Stop it. I almost came just looking at you."

The muscles she hadn't realized she'd been tensing relaxed, momentary trepidation replaced by a more urgent need. She wiggled her bottom, brushing his arousal.

He made a low sound in his throat and slid a finger inside her. Pinching her nipple, he added another digit, stretching her as slick moisture eased his entry. Forced to witness his every move, she bit down on her lower lip, embarrassed and aroused by her body's natural response.

He drove into her in a slow steady rhythm, his palm grinding a circle over her clit. Her breaths grew shallower with each inhale. Not accustomed to the dual stimulation, she had no defenses. She'd never been with a man experienced enough to remain in complete control, one intent on driving her to orgasm.

Needing an anchor, she bent her elbows and held onto the broad shoulders behind her. When her legs no longer supported her weight, she leaned against him, rested her cheek against his chest, and closed her eyes.

"No." He squeezed her breast, his grip tight enough to make her gasp. "I want you to watch." Shifting his hold to the neglected mound, he repeated the motion before flicking her nipple with his thumb.

Obeying his command, she lifted her lids and focused on her captor's reflection. She noticed his now ruddy skin, the protruding veins at his temples and along his arms, the stress lines bracketing his mouth. Against her back, his chest lifted and fell, the erratic motion mirroring her own. He teetered on a razor's edge, and she wanted nothing more than to make him fall.

Sliding a hand between them, she brushed his crotch. "Then stop playing."

With a curse, he freed her, grabbed both her wrists, and pinned them to the mirror. Using his body, he pressed her against the wall, flattening her breasts on the smooth surface. Imprisoned, all she could do was focus on each breath as he unbuckled his belt. She could feel the slide of metal against her bottom, the shifting cloth as he unzipped his pants and pulled them halfway down his hips.

A long, burning shaft slid between her thighs, the hard ridge brushing over her wet folds and reducing her legs to jelly. He pulled her toward him before pushing down on her lower back. She bent forward at the waist, aligning her forearms to the wall to brace her weight.

He reared back.

"Wait." With the last wisp of coherent thought, she magicked a condom from her cosmetic bag into her clasped hands.

Prying it from between her thumbs, he glanced at the packet. "Her Pleasure?"

"At least, I remembered." Thank goodness she'd stopped at the drugstore before coming here.

With a soft crackle, the packet tore. Pink foil landed on the floor between her feet. He pressed one palm above her bottom, the pressure forcing her to arch her back. As the head of his cock probed, he looped his free arm around her.

Her vision hazed when he parted her labia and circled. He pushed into her inch by torturous inch. His size would have been too much if not for the electric sensations pulsing from her clit. She rested her face on her wrists, watching their reflection out of the corner of her eye. His skin glistened, his dark hair draping over his forehead and cheeks. His lips were pursed, jaw tensed, brows drawn together. His blazing eyes seemed glued to her body, his intent gaze burning with unmistakable hunger.

He jerked his hips forward, burying himself to the hilt. She whimpered and shifted in a belated attempt to escape. Wet as she was, it'd been years, and she'd never been taken quite this way.

To her surprise, he remained still, allowing her to adjust. When the uncomfortable stretching eased, he pulsed his thumb over the bundle of nerves controlling her pleasure. Her straining muscles relaxed, her lids fluttering as dark spots marred her vision.

The palm at her lower back moved to mold over her breast. She heard her own high-pitched moans and sharp gasps, saw beads of sweat form on her forehead and chin. He continued to stimulate her while sliding in and out of her from behind. She couldn't decide what was worse—the burning friction of each penetration or the alternating pressure over her abused nipples. It didn't take long before her muscles began to spasm, the coil at her core winding tighter each time she drew breath.

"Leo, please." She had no idea what she was begging for. "It's too much."

He released her breast and removed his hand from between her legs, allowing the urgent yearning to ease for a split second before shifting to grip her waist. Then the slow, torturous impalement quickened to pumping thrusts, the steady deep penetration both torture and ecstasy.

The elevator echoed with her moans and his guttural cries, their breaths synchronizing as he continued to drive into her. Her hanging breasts swayed forward and back with each impact, her back arching in surrender and invitation. A deep fiery red ate into her vision. Her inner muscles clenched, her over-stimulated clit responding to the continued assault with urgent pulses.

"Fuck." Leo's harsh voice almost didn't register. His hips jackhammered, his cock pounding into her in an erratic rhythm. He pulled her to meet each entry, forcing himself deeper.

Then something inside her snapped. Her world blazed white.

Chapter Six

*S*eated on a marble elevator floor with a lumpy pink duffel cushioning his back, Leo struggled to wipe the smug grin off his face. With mirrors to his right and left, he could see how ridiculous he appeared with his chest bare and his hair a mess. Having just experienced the most mind-blowing sex of his life didn't mean he should gloat. After all, his life had become exponentially more complicated.

Wearing a T-shirt and panties from her bag, Cat lay curled up with her head on his lap. Glancing at the time on his BlackBerry, he tucked the curtain of hair covering her face behind her ear. Though his leg had gone numb from poor circulation, his lower back and butt muscles aching from recent activity, he couldn't seem to get the corners of his mouth to turn down. "Come on, kitten. Wake up. The elevator will be moving soon. Get some pants on."

Batting at his hand, she mumbled, "I'm awake."

He chuckled and pinched her cheek. He hadn't realized a groggy woman could still be sexy. "Sure, you are."

Sighing, he decided to allow her an additional two minutes. Aside from the clothing issue, everything was set for their departure. They'd cleaned up as best they could, using the remaining wet wipes in her cosmetics bag, and he'd disposed of all the trash with a flash of green flames. This whole fire-power thing was beginning to grow on him. With everything packed away, she'd claimed a need to rest her eyes and fallen into an exhausted sleep.

Having been the one who'd driven her into this weakened state shouldn't bolster his ego, but he was man enough to admit deriving significant satisfaction from the accomplishment. After all, trying to adhere to the ladies-first rule had damn near killed him. Glancing at their reflection, he noticed the crescent fingernail marks on his shoulders. He bent his neck to examine her sleeping form before tracing the hickeys he'd left on her nape and thighs. She shifted, a soft purr rumbling in her throat. And even though he was in no condition for round two, blood pooled in his groin.

Shit. The last thing he needed was to have her think him a sexed-up freak. With her cheek pressed against his thigh, her head was too close to his growing erection for comfort. "I'm serious about the jeans. Get up, so I can put my shirt on."

"Mmhmm...."

Grabbing her shoulders, he dragged her into a seated position. She yawned and rubbed her left eye with one fist, the act reminding him very much of her cat form. "We won't need to skedaddle for at least another fifteen minutes. I have low-grade precognition."

That would make surprising her with gifts somewhat difficult. He dug behind him and tossed the necessary item of clothing onto her lap. "Any other tricks you want to tell me about? Come on, you're already up. Make yourself presentable for the sake of my sanity, if nothing else." He couldn't stomach the thought of any other man seeing her in panties and a short T-shirt, which added irrational jealousy to his list of symptoms.

Casting him a sideways glance broadcasting pure feminine superiority, she rose and did as he asked, making sure to wiggle her gorgeous bottom as she huffed and puffed her way into slightly too-tight jeans. "Forget the shirt. You might as well show off those pecs."

Accepting the compliment with a nod, he flexed his legs to

stimulate blood flow. "I don't want to cause a riot in the lobby. Chicks can get weird about muscle definition. Then there's the matter of shoes and socks."

Her lashes fluttering, she sent him a disbelieving glare. "Doing chest presses at home alone is messing with your head. Join a gym. It'll give you a reality check."

He stood and grabbed his crumpled shirt. After sliding his arms into the sleeves, he focused on the buttons while suggesting in the most casual tone possible, "We can check out the one around the corner. I hear they give roommate discounts, now."

When he lifted his gaze, he found her leaning against one wall with her arms crossed. "So, you're not terminating my familiar contract? You said earlier I'm a free woman."

He wished he could read her expression. "Verbal concessions said in passing aren't legally binding. That said, it's your call. You're the expert."

She twisted her lips to the side. "We have such chemistry. You have no idea how rare it is. I'd hate to see all this potential go to waste."

He'd rather she weren't talking about their professional relationship. "I *do* have ethical issues with slave labor."

She rolled her eyes. "You pay me a very good salary, and I get a fifty-grand bonus in eighteen months."

His jaw dropped. "From a contract I've never even seen? Can my bank account handle it?" She'd be the one to ask, seeing as how she'd acted as the accountant for his inherited estate this entire time.

She strode over, his shoes and socks somehow materializing in her grasp. "Don't you read the financial reports I send you every month?"

He grabbed the proffered items and knelt to put them on. He'd created a filter, sending all those e-mails into an Outlook folder he never checked. "I've been busy. So, you want to stay roommates, huh?"

She sat on her knees in front of him. "Of course. If you

remember, Nonna's will left me half your house."

A valid point. "So we'll be like, you know, roommates who sometimes have sex with each other?" The words came out in a rush. He had no idea why his voice went high pitched at the end of the sentence.

Dimples decorated her cheeks. "I guess there's no one else I want to sleep or live with. As long as we can work out a more equitable division of chores...."

He jerkily nodded before he recalled the importance of masking enthusiasm. "Sure. I'll do whatever you want." He almost smacked his head. Talk about starting down a road toward being whipped.

Her Cheshire-cat grin confirmed his fate. She stuck out her hand. "You've got yourself a deal."

With a sigh, he met her palm with his. This might not be the best time to ask about her Thanksgiving plans.

FROSTY RELATIONS

Chapter One

*F*lexing her tired feet under the old wooden desk, Mina Mao stared at the image of a ten-foot-tall ice sculpture of Godzilla situated in the center of the World War II Memorial. In honor of tomorrow, the monster sported a Santa hat and held a Christmas tree between his two claws like a cigar. *The Washington Herald*'s headline read: "The Ice Maestro Wishes D.C. a Happy Holiday!"

Stifling a very unladylike laugh, she peered over the top of her computer screen to make sure no one stood in her office doorway. As the person in charge of monitoring everyone's Internet usage, she didn't want to set a bad example. But she'd been called in to Frost and Sons, LLP at 5:00 a.m. on Christmas Eve because of a stupid server glitch, and the problem hadn't resolved itself until half-past eight. By then, the law firm's staff had filtered in, forcing her to spend the next four hours addressing one computer crisis after another.

A combination of her Asian ethnicity and early-twenties age bracket somehow landed her the role of de facto tech troubleshooter despite her fresh-off-the-press bachelors in psychology, her official position in Human Resources, and her relevant experience being limited to planning LAN parties. Thank goodness, most problems here centered on jammed Escape keys, dislodged power and monitor cords, unapproved installation of screensavers released in the late nineties, and continued confusion over why Word Perfect shortcuts had disastrous effects in Microsoft Office.

Having snagged a spare moment to sit and enjoy a mug of tea, she couldn't resist googling what the infamous Ice Maestro had been up to. Checking out his newest creations had become a Hump Day bright spot. Smack dab in the middle of every boring week, Wednesdays used to arrive in tandem with extreme fatigue and disheartening loneliness. This winter, they came with a hilarious photo she could set as her desktop background to cheer her through an inbox full of unread e-mails.

Irreverent and audacious, the anonymous artist seemed to share her twisted and oftentimes politically incorrect sense of humor. Having just created the fifth masterpiece in his series of frozen art, D.C.'s most notorious vandal had gained a cult following and inspired an army of copycats. With #ICEMaestro trending on Twitter, these sculptures garnered more publicity than the president pardoning a Thanksgiving turkey.

She had always gotten a kick out of the lengths people went through to explain away the supernatural, and the 24-hour cable news cycle seemed to make reporters take guesswork to a whole new level of creativity. Last night, Fox News had hypothesized the sculptures were part of a government conspiracy to distract the public from yet another economic downturn, while CNN suggested the possibility of extraterrestrial activity.

She couldn't help but admire the artist's brass balls. While the younger subsection of the magical community laughed their butts off, the Mage's Council must be having a conniption fit. Made up of old-school warlocks and witches who still believed in secrecy, animal sacrifice, and pentagrams drawn in blood, the traditional hocus-pocus crowd tended to get cagey whenever overt displays of magic hit the mainstream press. Whoever created these marvels—one of which was a life-sized Edward Snowden mooning the White House—skated on thin ice.

Then again, the kind of raw, elemental energy it took to conjure these gigantic sculptures meant the perpetrator had enough power to give the Council a big middle finger. Reining him in might spawn more problems than letting the antics slide. After all, the most popular theory circling the blogosphere claimed these sculptures were part of a publicity stunt by Ben & Jerry's ice cream. Not a single news outlet had, as yet, used the word "magic."

A knock startled her. Jumping in her seat, she glanced up to find Angela, a near-sighted but competent legal assistant in her mid-fifties, striding over to her desk.

Mina breathed a sigh of relief as she minimized her Internet browser. "Hi there. Need something?"

"I know it's ten minutes before one, but the Comma Hitler moseyed home. Mind if this old gal gets a head start on Christmas?"

Though a Human Resources assistant with less than three months on the payroll, Mina had somehow inherited authority over the office staff after the HR Manager threw her hands up and quit a week into the administrator's five-week vacation. The fact that Mina made half the salary of the employees she supervised didn't seem to bother Jackson Frost the Second, the sixty-five-year-old curmudgeon of a managing partner who couldn't be bothered with running the place. "Your attorney turned over a new leaf when he got a girlfriend. Considering it's the end of a billing quarter, you'd think he'd stay at least until three."

Angela worked for Leo Difuoco, a junior associate with borderline OCD attention to detail and minor time-management issues. Up until a month before, he'd spent the last week of every month cramming in billable hours, leaving long after sundown on weekends and holidays. Lately, he spread his efforts into regular fifty-hour workweeks and always rode the elevator to the lobby by five.

"The lovebirds have a flight to the Virgin Islands in three hours. Word is, he bought a ring. If you don't need me, I'd rather spend more time with the grandkids."

Since the rumor mill tended to embellish, Mina didn't give

this piece of gossip much credence. What twenty-something in her right mind would want that kind of commitment? Cat Gato, the elder sister of Mina's close friend and Leo's special someone, was one of the most levelheaded witches on the planet. "Of course you can go. It's Christmas Eve. I'm surprised he managed to bribe you into not taking the day off."

Angela beamed. "This is his first vacation in three years. I couldn't risk the poor boy canceling because he needed to get his numbers up."

The firm had a simple rule regarding days off. The attorneys could skedaddle whenever they liked, as long as they earned the required amount of money each quarter. This policy applied to maternity leave, which might explain why only one out of several dozen associates was female. Since the consequence for not hitting their target included a pay cut then probation, followed by termination, some underperforming lawyers dragged their butts in even while running high fevers and taking vomit breaks. She'd be more sympathetic if most didn't goof off during the first three weeks of every month.

Curious, she pulled up the accounting module and groaned when she read the current tally. "Please tell me mini-Frost already left."

"No such luck." Angela looked over her shoulder. "The invoices I turned in put Leo's billings above his by a hair, so the Space Cadet is on a warpath. He's marching down the hallway as we speak. By the way, what possessed you to let Beth take his overflow work this week?"

Mina furrowed her brows. "Why? She's new, but I've heard she's good."

Angela rolled her eyes. "That girl spends half her day on the phone and makes careless mistakes. If she wasn't tall, blonde, and busty, she'd never have gotten through probation. With the testosterone crowd, all she needs to do is bend at the waist and elbow-squeeze her boobs whenever she drops off a document."

Sighing, Mina filed the information away and clung to a ray of hope. "Jack is young, male, and single. Maybe it'll work on him, too?"

Angela snorted. "He grew up with us as babysitters, and we call him the Space Cadet for a reason. Do you know what that brat cares about more than womanizing?"

Mina shook her head.

"Proper usage of spaces, periods, apostrophes, and commas." Mina couldn't help but notice Angela appeared gleeful over the imminent melodrama. Beth must have made an enemy at some point.

Feeling a headache brewing, she massaged the almost non-existent bridge of her nose. "You should go home. Don't let him charm you into transcribing his dictations." Most junior associates preferred to type their own briefs, but Jack clung to the antiquated clerical step by claiming it maximized productivity. Having seen his two-fingered keyboard pecking, she agreed.

"Don't worry. We've got a minute or two. The vending machine always sidetracks him." Leaning one hip on Mina's desk, Angela handed her a red envelope. "I ran in to give you this. We pooled some money and got you a Christmas present."

With a smile, Mina took the item. Since her parents no longer welcomed her in their home, it didn't hurt to learn she had a few new friends. "You all shouldn't have." She broke the seal, expecting to see a simple Hallmark card. When reality proved otherwise, she read the vellum invitation out loud. "Madame Eve invites you to a one-night stand. Your mystery date will meet you at the Castillo Capital Hotel at 7:00 p.m." She frowned. The name of this service provider sounded oddly familiar.

"You're so mature, we forget sometimes you're twenty-two. All the extra hours must be hell on your personal life."

She hated to look a gift horse in the mouth, but this sort of arrangement didn't quite fit in her comfort zone. "I don't know...."

Angela waved her hand in the air, dismissing Mina's as yet unarticulated protest. "It's just a date. If the guy's a loser, you have my permission to throw your drink at him. This gives you an excuse to play dress-up tonight."

The woman had a point. Mina couldn't think of a downside to showing up. Besides, she might as well get a head start on her New Year's resolution. She couldn't very well get over her ever-present childhood crush without trying other guys on for size. "I guess there's no harm."

The enthusiasm on Angela's kind face steeled Mina's resolve. She pulled her shoulders back. The time had come to stop acting like a sheltered, awkward girl and embrace the twenty-first century. If baby boomers could hook-up using eHarmony, she could, at the very least, accept a one-night stand as a holiday present. "All right. I'll give it a shot. Thanks!"

Walking out, Angela turned to give her a quick good-bye wave. "Merry Christmas, young lady. And welcome to our crazy family."

Slipping the invitation into her purse, Mina went over her mental to-do list. She needed to go home and change. Her holiday-themed getup had seemed fitting this morning, and she'd won quite a few giggles from the staff. But showing up in dark-green pants, a frumpy white button-down, and a red sweater vest would doom this date before she even got a word in. On top of that, she had plastic snowflake earrings dangling down the sides of her face and a Santa hat on her head.

Fingering her disheveled ponytail, she decided to take advantage of the early release to visit a salon. Her waist-length hair allowed her to go months between cuts, but she hadn't set foot in a beauty parlor for over half a year. A scalp massage should get her over the winter doldrums and set the right mood for the evening.

She picked up the phone to beg her cousin for a last-minute appointment when stomping footsteps alerted her to a possible change of plans. Two seconds later, an irate twenty-seven year-old man-child stormed into her office.

Her heart skipped a beat, as it did every time they crossed paths. Jackson Frost the Third had paired a charcoal-gray suit with a black French-cuffed shirt and silver tie. Diamonds and onyx twinkled from the platinum pin on his chest and the cufflinks at his wrists, both of which matched his black-faced, paper-thin Omega. His manners might be deplorable, but she couldn't find fault with his dress sense.

Wispy strands of silvery hair framed his bony face. Composed of sharp angles and planes, with thin lips and high slanting cheekbones, his features were too harsh to be handsome. Yet she'd seen countless women fall at his feet. Though she hated to admit it, if he paid her the slightest attention, he'd get the same result from her.

He opened his mouth, shattering his Prince Charming image into a million shards. "When were you going to tell me no one's coming to work tomorrow?"

In most other offices, it wouldn't have been necessary, since Christmas numbered among the ten official Federal holidays. Here, the overtime culture made the concept somewhat fluid. Having known Jack Frost since she'd worn diapers, his tantrums didn't scare her. Her family had served his in some capacity or the other for over three generations. Although Frost, Senior never openly practiced magic, he'd employed Mina's father as a familiar for three decades. As a result, she'd grown up next to their mansion in the comfortable caretaker's house.

Five years younger than the heir apparent, she'd worshiped Jack throughout her childhood and teens. Both their fathers had planned to make her his familiar when she grew up. But before leaving for college, Jack had washed his hands of magic, citing nonexistent powers as his reason.

As one of the few people who'd recognized this assertion to be an outrageous lie, she'd been confused and heartbroken. In hindsight, she thanked fate for his decision. He might not know it, but he'd given her the opportunity to live a normal life—to go to college and forge her own path. Had Jack not rebelled, her traditional *bàba* and *m?ma* would never have allowed her to break the mold, making her profession a consequence of birth rather than choice.

But since a psych degree meant next to nothing in America's anemic employment market, she'd ended up working for the Frost scion anyway. The lanky boy who'd rejected her in their youth had grown into the six-foot-tall, buff man scowling at her. "Well, Miss Mouse? You're the one who screwed me over, and you need to fix it. Get a secretary to come in tomorrow."

The nickname had stopped being cute when she'd turned six. It wasn't her fault her familiar form had been a black kitten with a white face and paws, or that her m?ma had adorned her pigtails in red ribbons for the majority of her childhood. The two factors combined to lend her a vague resemblance to a popular cartoon interpretation of mice. Since she hadn't shape-shifted or braided her hair in over a decade, the moniker no longer applied. He continued to use it for the sole purpose of annoying her.

Meeting his gray gaze, she lifted a challenging eyebrow. "If you somehow missed the tinsel in the lobby—tomorrow's Christmas. I said no to your request last week. Check your inbox."

His arms crossed, he glared at her. "You know I auto-delete HR e-mails. If it's important, you can move your skinny butt ten feet down the hall and tell me in person. I shouldn't have to hear this third hand from some crybaby new hire."

A vein pulsed on her forehead. "Your Outlook filters are not my problem."

He marched around her desk, planted his palms on her armrest, and bent down. With less than six inches separating them, it took significant effort not to flinch. He was much bigger than her, more so now that he'd piled muscles onto those broad shoulders and chest. But the physical intimidation distracted her far less than the scent of minty aftershave and Thierry Mugler's Angel.

Focusing on the silver flecks in his eyes, she forced herself not to look away or lean forward. He needed to learn neither intimidation nor attractiveness would get him any leeway with her. She might still have a slight crush on him, but she'd sooner walk over burning coals than let it show. Falling back on her very brief HR training, she muttered, "Please get out of my personal space. It's very unprofessional."

After trying to out-stare her for another ten seconds, he switched tactics. Rising to plop down on the empty chair opposite her seat, he targeted her with his best puppy-dog eyes. "I thought we were friends. How could you leave me high and dry at the end of a quarter?"

The man had been born a charmer. At its regular volume, his voice's low, smooth timbre could make any woman's blood pressure rise. In her more poetic, love-struck youth, she'd described his baritone as amber smoke layered over ice. At this particular moment, she'd call it a shot of whiskey on the rocks. It burned going down and left a nasty aftertaste.

Folding her hands on her lap, she straightened her spine. "Oh, please. We both know there's zero risk of your getting fired. You're here because your best bud beat your billings high score *and* ditched your annual Aspen trip to go to the beach. Get over your abandonment issues and find a different way to keep yourself occupied."

He stuck out his lower lip, widened his eyes, and scrunched up his nose. That expression used to get him extra servings of ice cream from both his nanny and the chef. On a grown man, it looked so ridiculous, she struggled to stem a giggle, which might be the reaction he was gunning for. "How is putting a nice chunk of change in some destitute secretary's pockets a bad thing? Where's your Christmas spirit, Mini Mao? I need your help."

It would have been more difficult to resist his manipulation had he not been equating her with a dead Chinese dictator for the past several weeks. After Miss Mouse failed to stick, he'd thrown new variations of her name around the office at regular intervals, and his current favorite had managed to make some headway with the lawyer crowd. "I asked. No one volunteered. Go home, *Frosty.*"

His eyes narrowed, the irises glinting like mercury. The temperature in her office dropped, the supernatural chill raising the hairs at the back of her neck. These physical manifestations of his power were why she'd called him a liar a decade ago. Elemental warlocks like the Frosts could only access their magic in its rawest state—conjuring fire, wind, water, and a whole host of other natural phenomena. For the most part, modern life stripped these abilities of utility, their potential to cause serious damage making any direct magical display risky and impractical. Familiars balanced them out by channeling the otherwise useless energy into more mundane cerebral tasks such as enchantments, illusion, telekinesis, teleportation, and foresight.

Though more efficient in animal form, a non-elemental witch such as her could process a modicum of leaked magic when in close proximity with either of the two Frosts, with or without the formality of an official agreement. The degree of compatibility between parties varied, and their two families happened to have the most reciprocal energy profiles.

Bàba once explained it as them being on opposed wavelengths, which created a rare and much sought-after synchrony among mages. She hadn't noticed it as a child, her bond with the younger Frost so natural it seemed part of her. But after he left for college, her magic had dwindled. Of course, it had rekindled with a vengeance after she landed this job.

Judging from Jack's mood, which had been foul for the entire three months she'd worked here, convincing him to leave her office empty handed might be a challenge. "It's nothing personal. Christmas is one of those pesky annual traditions when people care less about making money and more about being with family and friends."

He crossed his arms. "What good are you if you can't even get people to work on holidays?"

Well aware she lacked the necessary qualifications to run a firm this size, his comment hit a sore spot. It hurt, more so because the rebuke came from him.

Taking a deep breath, she counted backwards from ten in Mandarin. "My job isn't to make you happy. Since I don't like cussing people out at work, get out."

He stared at her for a long moment before sighing and scratching his head. "No need to get your panties in a twist. How many curse words do you even know?"

At this precise moment, she was tempted drop a few F-bombs and throw her stapler at his head. When the object in question lifted a millimeter into the air, she filled her lungs and tried to calm down. "I'm fine. Everything's peachy. Do you mind going away now?"

Instead of complying, he leaned back and lifted his feet onto the pile of folders on her desk. "I'm fucking sorry, all right? Can I at least make my argument? I practiced it and everything."

Chapter Two

*M*ina stared at Jack's surprisingly clean, stitched-leather soles, which she guessed cost him more than her month's paycheck. Though mad and tired enough to throw him out, she hesitated. He hated apologizing more than anything. The words must have felt like sandpaper in his throat. After over a dozen years as his neighbor, she'd long since concluded the icy, aggravating façade hid a decent-enough core. He just didn't seem to have a filter—at least not with her. "Fine. Go ahead, Counselor."

He grinned from ear to ear. This exact beatific expression had always made it impossible for her to hold a grudge. "If tomorrow's off the table, I could use some help right now. You know the firm's mutant version of Microsoft Word hates me."

She'd never understood how the same attorneys who snuck onto Twitter and Facebook every ten minutes couldn't seem to wrap their minds around database management systems, auto-fill templates, macros, and formatting styles. "I assigned Beth to help you today. She should still be here."

He steepled his fingers. "Which brings me to my very solid case. The bimbo you gave my work to puts two spaces after every period."

Wincing at his language, she lifted one finger in a plea for silence before glancing at the door. With a shake of her head, it slammed shut. She motioned for him to continue.

"Since she's got nice make-up and a decent dye job, I decided to let that one recurring mistake slide." He sounded so proud of his magnanimity, she struggled to keep a straight face.

Nodding, she attempted to feign commiseration. "I'm guessing there's more."

"I *always* say 'comma' before 'and.'" His apparent outrage prompted her to put her hand over her mouth to hide the curving corners. "You can listen to my tapes yourself. Beth *never* puts them in"

A huge proponent of Oxford commas, she could understand some of his pain. "I see. It's a training point, and I can sit down with her next week to discuss it, if you'd like."

"I'm not finished." He drummed the tips of his fingers against each other. "On account of her spray tan and mini-skirt, I tried to let the comma thing go. But then came the spelling mistakes, which, you know, wouldn't be there if she'd right-clicked on the red squiggly lines. Even I can figure that out."

Placing her elbows on the desk, she leaned forward and cleared her throat. "If you could stop commenting on female body parts, it would do wonders for my peace of mind. I'm still the firm's HR person."

He lifted an eyebrow. "What do you think I am, an idiot? I haven't directly mentioned a single one. My point is—I tried to give this chick allowances on account of her youth and...umm...other assets. Do you want to know what straw broke my back?"

"Nope."

"She can't add. There's a calculator on her desk, another one on her computer, and we're talking simple arithmetic, but none of her invoices come back correct. I don't know how it's even possible to screw up something like that."

She took a deep breath and inquired, "What did you do?"

He turned his hands palms up, his face the picture of innocence. "I very politely pointed out all her careless mistakes and told her to get her act together. Guess how she reacted."

"I'd rather not."

"Her face got all red, and she started the waterworks."

Picturing the amount of paperwork she had in store, she massaged her temples. "You made the poor girl cry?"

He rolled his eyes. "Please. After all the ladies I've dumped, I'm a walking crocodile-tears detector. She thought some sniffles would make me all awkward and gooey, but I got over that phase in middle school. To conclude, the typist you gave me has done nothing but slow me down. I deserve additional help."

He had a decent case—for any other day of the year. "Where is Beth now?"

"She hightailed it into the elevator after screaming, 'You can shove the two weeks' notice up your ass.' By the way, isn't it against company rules to leave without permission?"

Where did he think they worked—a slave camp? She slumped in her chair. "Then you're sh— out of luck. Everyone else is gone. You *do* remember today's Christmas Eve."

"*Eve* being the operative word. Today's a normal workday."

Why did nobody ever read her e-mails? "If you'd bothered to come to the last staff meeting, you'd know the partners gave everyone an early release. I sent out a follow-up memo about it." She tapped her wristwatch. "It's after one, which was when everyone had permission to leave. Most people ran off before noon."

He scowled. "What did I say about you telling me the important stuff in person? This is all your fault. Call someone back in."

The papers on her desk vibrated. He always brought out the worst in her. "I most certainly will not. And how did this turn into my fault?"

"You approved my secretary's vacation request last week. I wouldn't have gotten behind if some idiot hadn't messed up my work."

There were times in the day when hitting her head on the desk seemed like an awesome idea. They often coincided with visits from a certain silver-eyed blond. "Courtney had three months of leave on the books because of your repeated guilt-tripping. No decent person would have refused. Can't you get over losing to Leo this quarter and enjoy Christmas weekend?"

He canted his head, wearing a fake-debonair smile that would have made George Clooney proud. "What's with people and beaches? I don't get it. Call in Leo's girl—she knows what she's doing. It won't take long. All I need is help with one itsy-bitsy little filing."

Narrowing her eyes, she reached out with her mind and opened the door, a not-so-subtle hint. "Angela's got her entire extended family heading over for dinner. I couldn't drag her in if I wanted to."

"Then get me someone—anyone," he pleaded in a low, husky voice meant to melt hearts. Too bad she'd seen him practice it on enough girls to develop complete immunity. "I'll type the damn thing myself, but I need someone who can use the stupid accounting module."

She bared her teeth, not caring if the forced curving of lips approximated a smile. "Don't be such a Grinch. If this really isn't about your numbers, then you can send the bills out later. I refuse to call anyone back on Christmas Eve. Any other suggestions?"

He remained quiet for five whole seconds, which suggested he might be giving her rhetorical question some serious thought. "You're not doing anything this afternoon, are you?"

When loose papers floated in the air, she didn't bother keeping her errant telekinetic energy in check. Directing one sheet to hover against his jugular, she explained in her sweetest voice, "I'll have you know, I've got a hot date tonight. I need to get my hair done." Having wasted enough time, she logged off from the computer, grabbed her purse, and got up. With great difficulty, she managed to command all the hovering sheets back into neat piles.

Still seated, he lifted his palms in a gesture of surrender. "No need to resort to lying. You *should* get rid of those split ends, but I call bullshit on the date. You always spend Christmas weekend with your parents."

Her hand jerked over the leather strap, the pain of rejection too new for her to suppress the physical reaction. The holidays reminded her of how much her mistake had cost. "People change in five years, and the date is real." Or so she assumed. "Even if it weren't, I wouldn't spend the afternoon helping you win some stupid competition."

As she walked past him, he grabbed her wrist. The moment his fingers touched her skin, she froze. Very few people knew her magical specialty; he happened to be one of them. She was an empath, one powerful enough to sense emotion through touch. Since she believed in everyone's right to privacy, she avoided skin-to-skin contact. He'd taken great caution thus far to do the same.

His efforts had been unnecessary. She'd never been able to decipher Jack's emotions, in large part because he didn't seem to have a good handle on them himself. He felt—strongly, passionately, and intensely—but it was all jumbled together in an impressionist amalgamation he'd never bothered to tease apart. Since he couldn't make heads or tails of his own feelings, she couldn't interpret them without significant effort.

Amidst the chaotic mesh of restlessness and boredom, she sensed something she couldn't quite name. Beautiful in its complexity, a smoldering ember within his subconscious tempted her to reach into his mind—to tease apart the intricate weave of protectiveness and possessiveness to discover what he'd buried within.

But because of her vulnerability when it came to this one man, she twisted her arm out of his grasp and took a step back. Focusing on the more immediate problem, she placed her hands on her hips. He was bursting with magic—she couldn't find any other way to describe it. The immense influx of power that flowed into her the moment skin met skin sent her an inch into the air. "What the hell have you done? Trapping all that energy inside.... It isn't safe."

This time, his crooked smile lacked its usual mask-like

veneer. Swinging his legs, he vaulted to his feet. "Are you volunteering to help take the load off, or are you threatening to turn me in?"

He marched forward. She stood her ground.

"I'm not a mind reader. I don't know what you've done. I don't want to know." Considering the fleeting contact sent frost down her spine, she'd rather not guess. Faced with how much he needed her, the offer fell from her lips. "I'll stay...."

The hopeful puppy-dog impression returned in a flash. "To invoice?"

She wanted to grab his shoulders and shake him. "To make sure you don't explode from all the pent-up mojo you've stockpiled. Why did you let it get this bad?"

He patted her cheek, sending through another jolt and slamming her against an iceberg of garbled emotions. "You know the Winter Solstice does weird shit to elementals, and lots of weird planets came into alignment this year—the worst cosmic cluster-fuck in over a century, if daddy dearest is to be believed. It isn't a big deal, and the effect will wear off soon. If you're not going to work, then run along. Like you, I've got a hot date to prepare for."

He seemed so cool and calm. The man had an idiotic streak when it came to certain issues. Magic happened to be one of them. "You're not listening."

He picked her up by the waist and removed her from his path. "I don't when I'm not interested in what someone has to say," he called over his shoulder. "Relax. I've got everything under control."

☙

Jackson Frost the Third glared at the sleek, white-faced black cat seated by his keyboard. He should have known Mina would be in his office by the time he got back. She had stubbornness down to an art form.

He pointed at the door. "Scat. I told you I don't need this

voodoo shit. Trust me, your hair is in bad shape and in no condition for this damn date. Be a good kitty and go to the salon."

He shouldn't need to cajole. The woman had let herself go since she'd started working here. She cycled through the same frumpy old clothes, seemed to have developed an allergic reaction to all beauty products, and kept switching between two pairs of worn boots. She could be damn hot if she put her mind to it, but no. She'd let dark circles form under her huge brown eyes, shed at least three pounds her tiny frame couldn't afford to lose, and he could count the number of times he'd heard her laugh.

Of the two mages left in this empty office, he wasn't the one who required assistance.

Lifting the scrawny cat from the desk's clear-glass surface, he dropped her on the carpet.

She leapt onto his rolling office chair.

Turning, he pointed his index finger right above her judgmental little nose. "I do not have a magic repression problem."

Her whiskers twitching, she tilted her chin up and stared at him. Very few things got under his skin. Her silent treatment numbered among them. "I refuse to have an argument with a cat. At least have the decency to use your words."

She licked her lips. If she'd done that in her natural human form, it'd be sexy. As a feline, it was borderline cute. "How long do you plan on staying here?"

She tapped her face with a white paw, her familiar form's equivalent of a shoulder shrug.

Sighing, he picked her up, sat down, and set her on his lap. With a satisfied purr, she curled into a little ball. He could already feel the painful tension inside him ease, the bone-numbing chill funneling out in a consistent flow instead of sudden spontaneous bursts. Okay, maybe he'd been a little on edge these past months—not anything to worry about, but enough to make him uncomfortable. And so what if his skin might as well be splitting apart, or if his fuse had been short because of all the concentration it took not to freeze something by mistake?

He'd been handling the problem in his own way and had done a decent job of it, too. But as much as he hated to admit it, having a familiar around him did more good than all the stopgap measures he'd employed over the past five weeks. It's not like he *needed* her or anything. Her presence didn't hurt, that was all. He'd never allow himself to depend on anyone, least of all a bleeding-heart goody-two-shoes whose one accusing glare could make him feel like an asshole.

Being a tool was one thing. Wallowing in guilt, he refused to do.

Rolling his shoulders, he leaned against the webbed backrest and closed his eyes. As she worked her magic, he contemplated his evening, a much more pressing subject than his life choices. He'd fibbed when he'd told her he had a hot date. Having never met this mystery woman, he had no fucking clue how she'd rate.

Back on Halloween, he'd gifted his best friend a one-night stand through a mysterious online service run by Madame Eve. He should have known Leo would do the idiotic thing and shack up with the chick. Given, the man's new girlfriend had turned out to be a familiar, which had shoved Dumbo Leo out of the warlock closet and simplified their friendship, somewhat. But the couple had practically attached their hips together since then, and they were obnoxious in their unwavering contentment. To top it all off, Leo had ditched the annual Frost-Difuoco Aspen tradition to go to some stupid island with this crazy Cat person. What happened to bros before hoes?

Jack had never understood the point of beaches. All the sun ever did was make him sweaty and mess up his skin, and he couldn't seem to escape the sand. The crafty little granules got in his shoes and socks, dusted his clothes, and always found their way into his hotel room. He'd take the Swiss Alps over the Maldives any day of the week. Babes in bikinis, he could get behind, but since Leo never even checked out broads anymore, what was the damn point of going to the Virgin Islands?

In a word, life sucked. His best friend had turned into an absolute bore, the man's newfound happiness hurtling Jack's social life to a new low. He spent close to sixty hours a week as a glorified form filler, and ever since Mina showed up three months ago, he'd crashed and burned on every pick-up attempt.

Leo had the audacity last week to suggest self-sabotage, but what did that even mean? Jack was plenty horny—all day, every weekday, particularly between the hours of nine and five. He had no idea why the desire to bang someone dissipated the moment he left the office, or why he now preferred long walks in the snow to the D.C. club scene. But his dick's lack of action troubled him. He'd caught himself watching one of those testosterone supplement advertisements, wondering if "low T" might be the issue. Then he'd remembered he was two years over twenty-five, had more energy than he knew what to do with, and kept waking up from a recurring dream with a painful boner.

Hearing a meow, he stroked his hand over the cat's lithe body, sighing with relief at the current flowing from his palm to the smooth silky fur. So perhaps suppressing his magic had some negative side effects, making him moody, abrasive, and obliterating what little patience he'd once possessed. Being always on guard damned all his relationships before they even started, the crash-and-burn phase earning him a few hard slaps in the face. He should have done something about the problem after its escalation this year, but he'd thought he'd dealt with the planetary shit storm just fine. Since he'd undergone the genuine treatment, he suspected his initial assessment of his wellbeing might not have been 100 percent accurate.

On the topic of treatments, if he didn't get some serious bedroom action soon, he'd go insane. He'd arrived at this conclusion on the thirtieth day of his dry spell, which was why he'd signed up for the same one-night stand service he'd gifted Leo. But while his friend had gotten a confirmation in less than twenty-four hours, it had taken Madame two months to find Jack a compatible match. He'd received the couriered invitation this morning.

As long as he didn't follow in his harebrained friend's footsteps, Jack was on track to taking the edge off his sexual frustration with some no-strings-attached fucking after 7:00 p.m. tonight. The last time he'd graced the Castillo Capital's posh confines, he'd lost his best friend to a witch in a Catwoman costume—not one of his fondest memories. If he had any hope of salvaging this Christmas Eve, the elusive Madame better have sent him a date with comparable ta-tas.

Not that he considered big boobs an absolute requirement. He'd make exceptions as long as they were proportionate to the woman's build. One example he could think of was Mina. If she sprouted Double Ds, she'd appear disfigured. A mere three inches over five feet and possessing the narrowest shoulders he'd ever seen, the poor thing would be out of balance with a C cup. Judging from what he could make out despite her unflattering clothing, he hypothesized mid-sized Bs. On anyone else, this would be a deal-breaker, but hers looked about the right size and seemed plenty perky.

Yawning, he settled more comfortably into the seat and embraced the lulling haze. His mind wandered to the day Mina had showed up for an interview. In a departure from her current fashion slump, she'd worn a short skirt suit and glossy-black high-heeled pumps. On her way out, she'd swung by his office to drop off his major weakness—Shanghai White Rabbit Creamy Candy. He'd given her a high five and wished her luck.

That day, she'd stayed for no more than a few minutes and had left the door open. But in this foggy, slumbering vision somewhere between the dreams he could never recall and actual memory, he reached over her shoulder to shut it.

A mischievous grin on her face, she tilted her head back and met his gaze. "What do you want, Jack?"

He lifted his index finger and placed it over his lips. "Shh...."

Sashaying past him with feline grace, she shrugged off her jacket to reveal a crimson silk blouse. After draping the discarded garment over an office chair, she turned to face his desk. Placing her palms on the suddenly clutter-free glass, she threw him a sideways glance and motioned him over with her head.

The warmth of balmy fall allowed her to show off those smooth, toned legs. The tailored dark-green cotton hugged her ass's subtle curve, the back slit giving him glimpses of her creamy thighs.

Coming up behind her, he closed one palm over her mouth. She remained still, her small body trembling as he nibbled her neck. He grazed his teeth over the slender slope, pausing to suck a bright-red hickey onto her snowy skin.

Hearing a muffled moan, he clamped his fingers tighter as he slid his other hand under her skirt. Finding damp heat, he yanked down her panties. The scarlet lace fell to circle her four-inch heels.

Biting her earlobe, he whispered, "Stay quiet, or everyone will know I'm fucking you."

With one hand, he unbuckled his belt and freed his erection, his other arm still holding her in silent captivity. He kicked her legs apart and hiked up her skirt. Sliding his length between the creamy cheeks, he probed her wet opening with the tip of his cock.

A loud feline hiss jerked him out of the dream. Sharp claws dug into his thighs as the chair rolled back and hit the wall. The cat scampered off his lap. Rubbing his eyes, he tried to remember where he was. Once his mind regained focus, he glanced down at his crotch and noticed the very visible bulge. He could see why she'd reacted in a rather extreme fashion.

With a soft popping sound, the woman whose bare butt he'd envisioned appeared in front of him, her snowflake earrings swaying against the sides of her rosy face. At least she'd lost the Santa hat. "What the heck were you thinking about?"

The most honest answer would give her the wrong idea. After all, he wasn't *attracted* to her. He'd happened to be envisioning office sex with someone who bore a remarkable resemblance to her, at the same time he got an erection, while she'd been on his lap—all unrelated events. "My hot date tonight, obviously."

She scrunched up her cute little button nose. "Gross. Couldn't you have waited until I left?"

He checked his watch. More time had passed than he'd thought. "I'm a dude, and you were on top of me for two hours. If I'm not distracted, I start thinking about chicks. Why do you care?"

Her round pink cheeks turned an even darker shade. Considering she'd done him a huge favor, he decided not to comment. "I'm better now, by the way. You can go do your salon thing."

She tucked a loose strand of hair behind her ear and munched on her lower lip. He'd made her nervous. He wished he knew how he'd done it. She took a step back. "You're in better balance now, but you need a long-term solution. You know that, don't you?"

Why did she always have to be right? He found it annoying as all hell. "Can't I just buy you a steak once a week or something? God knows you need the calories." Sighing, he gritted out an admission, "I've already gotten better since you started working here. If we could come up with an informal arrangement, I'd be all set." This unprecedented level of commitment should have driven him to the hills. Instead, spending one night a week with her sounded pretty damn nice.

She hesitated for a moment before answering, "While I'm here, sure. But I'm leaving in the spring, so you should start searching for permanent help. Astrology isn't my thing, but I heard this amplification effect might last a few years."

For some reason, her words felt like a sucker punch. "What do you mean, you're leaving?"

She fiddled with the ponytail that had draped over her shoulder and fell in a straight line down her chest. "I turned in my notice before my boss went on vacation. She asked me to keep it on the down-low until she came back."

His throat went dry. "If you've got a better offer, I'm sure Dad will match it." And if the old man didn't, Jack would put his own trust fund to good use.

She shook her head. "It's kind of a career change. This whole full-time job, taking grad school classes at night, and dumping my paycheck into tuition isn't working out so well. I applied to join Teach for America back in October, and I got accepted. The pre-service training starts in May, so I gave the firm until April first. I want to do some traveling before I move to Detroit."

"Detroit? What the fuck is in Detroit?" He hadn't just shouted, had he?

Her brows drew together. "Low income schools? They'll help me get loans to finish off my master's so I can actually go into practice, and I've always been interested in teaching. Anyway, you shouldn't count on me hanging around."

Glancing at her own watch, she edged toward the door and sent him a hasty wave. "I've got to go. Merry Christmas, Jack. And have fun on your date."

Chapter Three

*D*ulcina Gato, who preferred to go by her nickname *Sweets*, lifted a pair of rusty scissors in the air. "So the guy seriously had a boner? That's so messed up."

Mina rolled her eyes at their joint reflection. "I know, right? And since I'm an empath, I could sense him getting, you know, all hot and bothered. Whoever he was fantasizing about, she turned him on big time. I don't know how he could think about sex when he's on the verge of exploding from too much unused magic. "

Sweets snorted. "Men—warlocks or human—they care about one thing." She picked up a handful of Mina's hair. "Ready?"

Mina swallowed. "Are you sure you know what you're doing?"

Using the scissors, Sweets pointed at the set of combs and razors peeking out from a battered leather sleeve. "Can't you feel the mojo rolling off my grandmother's enchanted tools? These babies are idiot proof."

Since not even her cousin could squeeze her in after 3:00 p.m. on Christmas Eve, Mina's options had been limited enough to make her take a gamble. "But you *have* done this before?"

Patting her shoulder, Sweets bent at the waist and squinted one eye. "I cut Shelley's hair all the time. She hates leaving the house, remember? Okay, yours is too long. You need to stand so

99

I don't get a backache."

This idea seemed worse by the minute. Rising to her feet, Mina made a pinching motion with her index finger and thumb. "All I need is for you to take off the ends—nothing fancy."

Her friend's mock salute didn't bolster Mina's confidence. "Your hair is safe with me. Your head is another story."

Mina closed her eyes. "Very funny. Do it already, will you? The anticipation is killing me."

She heard a snip, followed by "Oh, wow."

Her lids snapped up. "What do you mean, 'Oh, wow'?"

She saw the answer for herself. Scissors and razors slashed around unguided in the air, slicing off huge chunks of her tresses in the process. Her friend stood several steps away, staring at the spectacle as if seeing the phenomenon for the first time. Since moving risked impact with pointy magical objects, Mina glared at the culprit's reflection in the mirror. "I thought you said you'd done this before."

Sweets's expression lacked any hint of guilt. "Okay, I lied. Shelley's grandmother is the actual owner of these puppies, and she always uses them on herself in the bathroom. Since her hair turns out fine, I figured they'd work on you, too."

Her hands fisting, Mina hissed, "How do you turn the darn things off?"

When Sweets answered with a shrug, Mina began to question how they got along so well at night school. Yes, they happened to both descend from familiars, but that was about all they had in common. Having earned her bachelor's online, Sweets was a year younger and a decade less mature.

Mina's expression must have approached homicidal, since Sweets elaborated. "Shells explained how it works. I put the kit on top of your outfit, it figured out what cut would suit you best, and it's doing its thing. When it's done, it'll stop. There's nothing to worry about."

Since much less of her hair had dropped to the plastic-covered floor than she'd feared, Mina embraced the madness. "Fine, but talk about something to distract me. I'm this close to making a run for it."

Sweets's gleeful smile suggested this might have been her plan from the get-go. After all, she'd turned Mina into an immobile prisoner of the enchanted hair-cutting apparatus. "So, why do you still have a crush on Boner Boy?"

The question confirmed her suspicions. "I don't."

"You were about to stand up your date tonight until I practically beat down your door. You should thank your lucky stars Shelley had a vibe about this."

Narrowing her eyes, Mina voiced an ongoing suspicion. "Right...Shelley. Remind me, who's the one with foresight? You or this mutant elemental earth mage who shouldn't have the ability to begin with?"

The witch's golden cheeks colored. "Who are you, Veronica Mars?"

"If I figured it out, so will Enforcement. Precog familiars are supposed to register with the Council. Rumor has it they've been hunting one for a year."

Sweets stuck out her tongue. "You're dodging my question. I can tell you've been around lawyers all day."

"They're the boring kind. All they do is write briefs and fill out forms to send to the Patent Office. You can't find a nerdier cluster of people in D.C."

Her friend waved away the clarification. "Again, more distraction tactics. We were talking about Boner Boy."

"Can you stop calling him that? His name's Jack."

"Touchy, touchy. Okay, so what did this Jack do back in the day to win your undying devotion?"

Mina focused on not flinching as scissors and combs hovered far too close to her face for comfort. "Nothing. He was just nice. We both had very distant parents, I guess, so he always treated me like his annoying little sister. He still does, which is why I decided to move on years ago."

Sweets strolled around Mina's four-hundred-square-foot studio apartment. The small room was in an up-and-coming neighborhood in South D.C., and she counted every time the hot water worked as a small miracle. Stopping at the huge collection of snow globes on her single chest of drawers, Sweets remarked, "Holy shit. This is some serious juice. Boner Boy give you these?"

While Mina's brother and Jack had always accompanied their fathers on various trips throughout her youth, she'd never left the tri-state area. Travel cost money, which her parents preferred to spend on their son. Perhaps noticing the well-hidden hurt from the unequal treatment, Jack had returned from each sojourn with a souvenir. Each globe contained an actual miniature snowstorm, all of them still brewing, even though the first one had been conjured more than fifteen years ago.

She recalled the afternoon he'd gifted her the final one. She'd been filling her parents' beat-up old minivan with her luggage when he'd appeared out of the blue to wish her luck before she left for college. Having flown in from Boston, he'd given her a globe modeled after the Maparium. To this day, it remained her favorite present. "Yeah, those are all his. They're how I know he's nice guy, but it's hidden so deep I sometimes forget."

Flicking her shoulder-length hair back, Sweets turned, placed her hands on her hips, and fluttered her long, dark lashes. "My my, Ms. Mina Mao. I think you're in love with the man."

Mina snorted at the horrible impression of a southern belle. "It's platonic love. I told you, he treats me like a baby sister."

"Did your big brother ever give you presents, or did he spend his days putting bubble gum in your pigtails and stealing your allowance?"

Tony had done both—and once they grew up, it had gotten even worse. Shuddering at the memory, she remembered why she needed to get out of the city. As much as she loved her brother, the situation had become too difficult. "Trust me, Jack and I might share a...bond. But he's never seen me that way.

"I thought you said you could never figure what he's feeling, since he doesn't seem to know himself?"

Her friend had a point, but she refused to go down that path. After watching him dump a score of girls over the course of a decade, she'd learned that falling for a Frost was a recipe for heartbreak. "I thought you came here to convince me to see this one-night stand through?"

Sweets lifted her index finger into the air. "I said it was imperative you *go* on this date. What happens once you get there is up to fate."

"I'm pretty sure it's up to me."

Her friend waved away the objection. "Same diff. Besides, you need someone to wipe away the bad taste of your ex-boyfriend. He poisoned the pool for the rest of mankind, and it's not healthy."

Mina avoided alcohol for a reason. Because of a twisted quirk of genetics, it took a single glass of wine to turn her into a babbling idiot, which was how the meddling witch in front of her had gleaned the details of that unfortunate mistake. "Trust me, I got over the dude when I broke up with him two years ago."

The flurry of activity around Mina's head calmed down somewhat. To her relief, she'd lost two inches of actual length at the most. Layered and wispy tendrils replaced the straight heavy glob. The scissors had flown back into the case, but two combs continued to battle with her slippery locks. With the coast clear, Sweets strode toward her. "When was the last time you got laid?"

"What are you, my therapist? I can't have sex without skin contact, which triggers my one useless power. Trust me, nothing sours the mood like sensing a man's emotions when you're locking lips."

"A guy should be thinking positive and yummy things at that particular moment. If he isn't, he's the one with the problem."

She'd managed to handle the physical side of her relationship with Michael because he'd never cared much about anything. When it came to sex, the overwhelming reaction she'd detected was indifference. "I guess there's something wrong with me."

"Yes. You have shit taste in men—or, well, man."

"What is this? Interrogate Mina Day?"

"Nope. It's Slap-Some-Sense-into-Mina Day. For an empath with a psych degree, you've got some serious self-esteem issues. Just because the first guy you dated was a borderline sociopath doesn't mean you're doomed for all eternity."

Sweets had a point. Since Mina suspected the woman to be a powerful, albeit closeted, foreseer, she gave today's advice significant weight. "Okay. Enough. I already said I'm seeing the night through, barring unforeseen circumstances. I packed condoms and everything."

Grinning from ear to ear, her friend eyed the combs, which had wrangled Mina's hair into an intricate French braid and coiled the tail to form a chignon at the back of her head. "I have to say, this kit's a bit old school, but it has good taste. You're going to knock your date off his feet."

ભ

Chicks never showed up on time. Perhaps punctuality was a trait unique to the Y chromosome, or maybe some girly magazine once advocated tardiness as a type of power play. Either way, Jack could never count on a woman's arrival without going through the trouble of dragging her there.

Back in his freshmen year of college, he'd decided only losers waited for dates to show up. He made a point to avoid such a disadvantageous first impression—even if it meant spying on a hotel entrance through a pair of binoculars while still ensconced in his Lamborghini convertible. Though it looked weird next to the piles of dirty snow on the sidewalk, he'd put the top down. The cold affected him in a peculiar fashion. Instead of slowing him down and causing discomfort, lowered temperatures pumped him full of energy and lifted his spirits.

If he'd had more notice, he would've hired some schmuck to stand outside with a video camera so he could watch his date's progress from the comfort of his hotel room. But Madame Eve hadn't given him the courtesy of advance warning. For some reason, when he'd called his trusty private eye earlier this afternoon to request his services, the man had burst out laughing and hung up—another item to add to his growing list of why holidays were evil. Christmas messed with people's heads.

He could, he supposed, wait inside the hotel like every other idiot, for once, but the consequences could be dire. What if this woman turned out ugly—or even worse—ditzy? Seated inside, extrication would be a huge pain in the ass. If she didn't take the hint, as women with limited intelligence tended to do, he'd have to resort to acting offensive and rude. While he had no moral objection to being a dick, coming up with insulting verbiage took more effort than one might think.

Whoever came up with the whole "don't judge a book by its cover" saying lived in La-La Land. He could learn a great deal about his potential date based on her appearance. For one, at tonight's below-freezing temperature, it'd take a certain level of stupidity to show up with no leg or head coverage. Considering the sheet of slippery ice on the sidewalks, the woman had better be wearing sensible shoes, preferably with Louboutins stashed in her Chloë purse.

And then, of course, the hotness factor came into play. He wouldn't bother getting out of his car if she didn't score at least a six out of ten while wearing a coat. Because of his preference for winter activities and vacation spots, one of his many pet peeves was skimping on outerwear. Taking couple shots and posting them on Facebook numbered among the top reasons why most people even bothered dating, and frumpy clothing made for crappy photos.

Besides, this activity distracted him from the weird edginess that had plagued him all afternoon. He couldn't fathom what caused it. It felt as if insects crawled under his skin, and his mood shifted without warning between annoyance, irritation, and nausea-inducing despair. His knuckles itched, his hands tensed for no reason, and his face turned warm at random intervals. He didn't know why, but googling Teach for America and finding out they had a Washington, D.C. corps managed to silence the roaring in his ears, but he'd still been overwhelmed by the urge to pace.

And he never paced. He couldn't understand the point of marching back and forth like a caged lion while glancing at the phone every two minutes. He'd no idea whose call he waited for, or whose number his index finger twitched to dial, but he refused to surrender to the medley of emotions tying his stomach into knots. His shoulders had gotten all achy, his neck muscles stiffer than usual. Since all masseuses in the city had decided to take today and tomorrow off for no good reason, he'd been grateful to have this one-night stand as a distraction.

A piece of white paper flitted into his line of vision, landing on his lap. Scowling, he put down his binoculars and yelled after the middle-aged woman who'd apparently just pulled up in an old-model Prius. "You're giving me a ticket? It's Christmas Eve."

She turned to face him and pointed at a sign two cars down.

Frowning, he squinted at the fine print. As luck would have it, it happened to be the third Wednesday of the month between 6:00 and 9:00 p.m. Damn the city's messed up parking rules. "But I'm *in* the car."

"It says no stopping, not no parking. You're in front of the Canadian Embassy. Please move your vehicle."

Located off the National Mall and around the corner from the Archives Metro Station, the Castillo Capital had a great view of the Smithsonian Cathedral and happened to be adjacent to a number of diplomatic missions. "Give me a break. Where am I supposed to go?"

"The hotel has parking."

Reaching over the door, he pointed at the less-than-four-inch clearance between his car and the road. "The angle into the underground lot is too steep. I'll scrape the car. And they won't let me park by the entrance unless I give up my keys. You know valets can't be trusted."

Her nostrils flared. She closed her eyes for two seconds before responding, "There are spots around the corner."

"*Those* creepy alleys?" D.C.'s relatively recent gentrification meant very few feet separated shady and posh neighborhoods. "Do you want me to get mugged?"

"Not my problem." She squinted, pressed a few buttons on her handheld machine, which spat out another ticket. Walking over, she dangled it in front of his face. "Your tags are expired."

Snatching it, he pressed the ignition button and peeled out. As he rounded the block and headed toward the National Archives, a sudden psychic tug drew his attention. Even though Mina had never officially signed on as his familiar, he could always sense when she came near. A comforting warmth curled in his gut, the air currents altering in a way he could never describe in words. He hadn't given the phenomenon much thought. Trying to explain awesome things took the mystery out of life.

His rendezvous forgotten, he continued forward until he spotted a feminine silhouette in the distance. He couldn't see much, but his magic, sensing an outlet, zeroed in with laser-like precision. He leashed the current of power, parallel parked, and shut off the headlights. It'd be damn fun to jump onto the sidewalk and yell boo.

Grabbing his handy-dandy binoculars, he zoomed in on Mina. She'd just exited the Metro Station. Wearing heelless black boots, she drowned in an oversized, shapeless maroon coat that reached halfway down her calves. Adding to the fashion disaster was a faux-fur-lined hood that reminded him of the obscuring cowl in the video game *Assassin's Creed*. Hands shoved in the pockets, she marched forward, not looking left, right, or back. Her breath created a white mist in the cold air, her nose and cheeks an adorable red.

He frowned as he watched three Asian men follow her out of the station and onto the sidewalk. The one hanging farthest back wore a knee-length wool coat and sported a black dragon tattoo that covered his neck and half his face. In front of him marched a tall, skinny dude wearing a leather jacket, his ears and nose serving as a walking spiky-jewelry advertisement. The muscled-up guy closest to her appeared normal enough. Short and beefy, he wore a nondescript Old Navy hoodie and baggy jeans.

Smart girl that she was, she must have sensed something fishy about the Chinatown crew as well. She hastened her footsteps, which might not be the best of ideas since she was heading into a darker section of the street. Drawing her shoulders forward, she cast a furtive glance at her pursuers.

The men closed in until two of them bracketed her on the left and right. She broke into a run. Dumping the binoculars, Jack jumped over the car door and sprinted toward her. His heart choked in his throat as the bodybuilder dude grabbed her by the head and pulled her kicking body into a dark alley.

Fear coiled and froze into cold rage. One scratch on her and he'd bury the city in ice, if that's what it took to make them pay.

Chapter Four

*H*er scream muffled by a ham-fisted hand, Mina's stomach lurched at the foul odor of stale cigarette smoke, sweat, and cheap whiskey. Eyes watering, she stomped her heel on her assailant's foot and jabbed her elbow into his stomach.

The beefy man grunted. *"Biao zi."* His hold loosened enough for her to fill her lungs. Capitalizing on the element of surprise, she grabbed the Taser in her coat pocket, twisted her torso, and stabbed it into his upper arm. With a choking sound, the thick-necked peon crumpled to the ground.

"Biao zi yang de," she muttered under her breath. Served him right for calling her a bitch.

Turning to face his fellow gangster wannabes, she considered her options. The Council frowned on public use of magic, but her weapon had dispelled its single charge. Each man was twice her size. Face-to-face, she doubted her self-defense classes would do much good. Deciding to bide her time, she tried to channel a scared damsel in distress and failed. "What do you idiots want?"

Because of her height, men tended to underestimate her. Until this moment, she'd never considered it an advantage. With a leer, nose-ring dude lurched forward and grabbed her by the shoulders. Since her strongest ability required touch, she let him shove her against the side of a building. Thank goodness the hood separated her hair from the dirty brick. Her attacker hadn't worn gloves, which simplified matters.

"Don't be stupid, *mei-mei*." His rotten breath brought tears to her eyes, the stench triggering a gag reflex. His grin widened, displaying a shiny golden tooth. "Keep fighting, and I'll hurt you worse."

She rolled her eyes. The guy couldn't be older than twenty. "Little sister, my ass. If you have a beef with Tony, go after him. Trust me, anything I've got that's worth more than a hundred bucks, he's already stolen." She'd known this day was coming, ever since her brother broke into her apartment and grabbed anything he could sell. It was why she carried around a Taser.

Her captor's grip tightened. If he kept going down this route, she'd be tempted to get nasty. "Your *Ta-ge* took our product on credit and skipped town. Now your family owes us ten grand."

Leave it to her drug-addict big brother to do something this stupid on Christmas Eve. "Do you really think I have that kind of money?" she spat back. "Even before the *sha gua* stole my ATM card and cleaned me out, my account never got over four digits."

The tattooed older man stepped forward and patted her cheek. The lecherous gleam in his eyes made her thankful black leather covered his fingers. "America has allowed you to forget yourself. Tony is your elder—the future leader of your family. Calling him an idiot is not a woman's place."

When it came to gender roles, some second and third generation immigrants acted like they were still fresh off the boat. Considering recent events, she couldn't respect her brother if she tried. "Kiss my ass."

The man's lips firmed into a thin line. "Your bàba and m?ma too have forgotten what matters. With their fancy house and car, they could have paid when we threatened to kill their only son. But instead, they called the cops, telling us they refused to waste more money on the no good *yanse lang*."

She gained newfound respect for her father, though she couldn't imagine him saying "man whore" in any language. "It's not their house or car, moron. Bàba works for a rich white guy.

And why do you think I'll pay?" If she had the money, she might consider it. But she couldn't cobble a grand together, let alone ten.

"We don't." His snake-like voice slithered down her spine, the unarticulated threat coiling around her neck and threatening to cut off air. "Your father will pay to save his hardworking, dutiful daughter—especially once we send him a video of our men taking turns with your cunt."

Stifling the urge to vomit, she redirected her attention to the walking human piercing who held her immobile. The magical community had one hard and fast rule about psychic attacks—always give at least one warning. "If you don't let me go, I'll fuck you up so bad you'll be screaming in a cell for days."

The jackass hooted out a laugh and closed his bare hand over her throat. "I'll have fun breaking you."

She wished she could say the same. Using the bruising point of skin contact, she shoved her power into his mind. Sifting through the maelstrom of jealousy, hatred, and arousal, she searched and found the core of all his fears. Amplifying the dark, slimy abyss, she folded the terror over itself. Bile coated her tongue as her attacker screamed and lurched away. He scrambled back over the frozen dirt on his hands and ass, the bottoms of his jeans and sneakers leaving indentations on the ice-slicked ground. Coughing, she struggled to catch her breath before turning to face the last man standing.

The gangster looked her up and down before remarking in a too-calm voice, "*W? po.*"

She massaged her throat. "I prefer psychic to witch, but if it helps get the message across. Why don't you take your boys home and tell your boss to let this one go?"

In response, he pulled a black hunk of metal out of his coat pocket and pointed the barrel in her direction. "Or we can work out a creative way for you to pay off Tony's debt—without touching me, of course."

This one proved to be the single member of the club with any brains. Good thing he thought she was a one-trick pony. She'd be in deep shit if she hadn't spent an hour this afternoon stockpiling Jack's magic. "Move the hell out of my way, *ji bai*."

One corner of his mouth curved up. Then he pointed the weapon at her leg. Before he could pull the trigger, she aimed a telekinetic blast at his wrist. Howling with pain, he dropped the pistol. With a flick of her head, she sent it skidding straight into the gutter. Threat eliminated, she lobbed another psychic blow between his legs. More drained than she'd anticipated, she didn't wait to see how much damage she'd done.

Sprinting toward the lights at the alley's entrance, her heart pounded as she heard footsteps behind her. She'd never hated her short legs more. Curiosity winning over caution, she twisted her head and glimpsed Tattoo Guy limping in pursuit. She must have hit his thigh instead of his balls. Quickening her pace, she turned and slammed into a charcoal-gray suit.

Despite her significant momentum, the solid masculine form didn't budge or express any signs of pain. The familiar scent of Angel, laced with snow, permeated her next breath. Then a pair of strong arms wrapped around her waist and squeezed tight.

All muscles relaxing, she tilted her head back and met worried silver eyes. "Jack?"

His familiar crooked smile steadied her adrenaline-fueled, topsy-turvy world. "I was about to play knight in shining armor, but you went all witch-fu on the bastards. What are you doing here?"

Remembering the man chasing her, she turned...and watched her assailant slam full speed into a newly materialized wall of ice, the thudding impact putting him down for the count. In the blink of an eye, the conjured barrier collapsed into a pile of powdery snow. "Please tell me you didn't kill him."

His arms manacling her, Jack's chest vibrated. "You're such a law-abiding sweetheart. A little concussion never hurt anybody."

She glared at him. "What if he mouths off...?"

He smoothed one palm up her back and yanked down her hoodie. "And says what? That he crashed into a non-existent block of ice after attacking a witch? Where were we? Oh, yes. What brings you to this part of town, and when did you learn the word 'cunt' in Mandarin?"

Did she say ji bai out loud? "The guy started it. And I have a date tonight—or I did. I'm so late, the poor man's probably gone."

"And where was this hunk supposed to be, if you don't mind me asking?"

Put off balance by the entire sequence of events, she furrowed her brows. "At the Castillo Capital down the street, but I'm less in the mood to meet him now than I was before." Sighing, she beamed a smile at the man crushing her against his chest. "What are the chances I can charm you into giving me a ride home?"

He angled his head from side to side. "I could be persuaded. But I'm curious—you wouldn't by any chance know who Madame Eve is, would you?"

"Umm...." Then the pieces fell into place. "*You're* my one-night stand? Thank goodness. I'm not missing anything, then."

He placed one hand over his heart, his other palm remaining in its initial spot at her lower back. "You sure know how to boost a guy's ego. Trust me, you lucked out on this anonymous match. I'm hot stuff."

Giggling, she reached up and patted his shoulder. "Don't get me wrong—you're a good-looking guy. But I'm glad to know this night was never going anywhere."

He caught her chin. Her eyes widened at the cacophony of emotions soaring into her. What the hell went on in his head? "You're the empath. How do I want this to end?"

Her throat closed up as possessive tenderness coiled around her, the intensity so palpable she sensed it as heat. Everything about the way she defined her relationship with him threatened to unravel. Not ready to face a truth that became clearer with each passing second, she turned her face and broke contact. "I don't think you know."

He chuckled. "That sounds about right." Releasing her, he

stepped to the side, swept out his arm, and took a bow. "My white horse awaits, Ms. Mao."

Cऔ

"I'm sorry, but that monstrosity's got to go." His nose wrinkling, Jack motioned at her coat from the driver's seat as the Lamborghini's scissor doors lifted. "Aside from being butt ugly, it touched those gross people. I don't want gangster cooties on my baby."

Relieved he'd reverted to his usual difficult self, she undid the buttons before pulling her arms out of the polyester-wool blend garment. With a cap-sleeved modified *cheongsum* underneath, she had a hard time combatting hypothermia. "You need to put the top up if you don't want me to turn into a Popsicle," she muttered through chattering teeth, thankful for the leather boots that reached just under her knees.

For some reason, her companion seemed frozen in place, his quicksilver eyes glued to her chest area. Concerned about a possible tear, she surveyed her front and noted nothing out of place. The red dress had a mandarin collar that buttoned under her chin, so no cleavage showed. The silk hemline brushed the top of her knees, which were covered in black cotton tights. A re-appropriated bridesmaid's outfit, it was on the fitted side since it had been tailored to her measurements. Given a choice, she'd have chosen something with more breathing room, but Tony had stolen most of her clothing. Thank goodness for the few garments she'd forgotten to retrieve from the dry-cleaner's.

Shrugging off Jack's odd reaction, she rolled up her coat and placed it next to his briefcase on the floor under the glove box. Sliding onto the soft leather seat, she blew into her hands. Having short legs meant she had plenty of room left. "Umm.... Can you get a move on? I'm dying here."

"Where am I taking you, exactly?" With the push of a button, the doors lowered and the convertible's metal roof projected out of the rear compartment to form a seal on the windows and windshield.

"Home, of course." Where else would she go? "Or do you still want to go for drinks at the Castillo?" She couldn't wait to shower, change, and sleep, but she'd persevere if he insisted. She doubted he would. After all, he'd come here expecting sex, not a platonic chat with a friend and co-worker. It would make the most sense for him to drop her off and go try his luck with someone else.

The engine purred to life. Since the seat and backrest emitted a welcome heat, she sighed with contentment. Once she warmed up, she grabbed her coat and rifled through the inner zippered pocket to unearth some wet wipes.

"I wondered why you didn't have a bag."

Grateful nothing other than her face and hands had been exposed to her assailants' grasping fingers, she scrubbed the problem zones in an attempt to banish tonight's memory. While she'd never doubted she'd get out of the jam safe and sound, being pawed at by those men left an icky psychological residue. "Purse snatching is back in vogue, and my neighborhood is in the beginning stages of up-and-coming. The big breast pockets are why I bought this coat."

As the car careened onto Pennsylvania Avenue, he drummed his fingers on the steering wheel. "Since I got distracted by all the Chinese cuss words, I missed some of the conversation. You'll have to fill in the gaps."

Her spine snapped straight. "Since when did you learn Mandarin?"

"I went through a *Firefly* addiction phase in college. Joss Wheedon had all the characters swear weird, so I read up on the translations."

"Cool. What did you think about the movie—?"

He took a sharp turn, the momentum launching her against the door. "Stop stalling and tell me what kind of trouble Tony got you into."

Buckling the seatbelt, she clutched the damp wipe in her hand. "It's none of your business. Everything is under control."

"Like fuck." He'd never used a tone this harsh with her before. "You got a magical boost by accident this afternoon. If not for me, you would've been in over your head. Let's skip to the part where you tell me how your deadbeat brother screwed shit up."

Until tonight, she'd seen him annoyed, irritated, and peeved, but always with a dose of nonchalance. The pure cold rage lacing his voice took her by surprise. "You know Tony. He's had problems ever since I first turned into a kitten. It's why he'd never finished high school, gotten a job, or moved out."

He rounded the next corner several miles too fast. "So he wasn't born with magic. Boo fucking hoo. He has no idea how lucky he is. So what happened—he moved on from alcohol and Ecstasy and graduated to heavier shit?"

She hadn't known the Frosts had been aware of her family's problems. "I don't know. I didn't even know about any of the drugs until a year ago. Mam? found white powder in his room. He swore it was nothing—some stuff he'd held onto for a friend. My parents asked me to come over and make sure he told the truth." An empath served as a walking lie detector. Emotion betrayed the verity or deceit of each answer.

"Since the bastard's been popping pills for over a decade, I'm guessing they gave him the boot."

Sinking into the cozy hot seat, she shook her head. "I should have known they both wanted me to lie. He's their only son—the offspring meant to carry on their name. They didn't want to hear or see the truth. When I told them he was a two-faced drug addict, he turned the tables on me—said horrible things about a mistake I made in the past, proved that I'd disobeyed and dishonored my family." Remembering the pain of rejection, the disappointment on her parents' faces, she closed her eyes. "They disowned me, not him. I haven't seen them in eight months."

When her audience burst out laughing, her burning lids popped open. "What about my messed-up life do you find so hilarious?"

His shoulders heaving, he slowed the car down. "Let me

guess—he told them you have a boyfriend and that you'd slept with the schmuck."

She puffed out her cheeks. "I *had* a boyfriend, and how did you guess?"

He blinked away tears of mirth. "Colorful vocabulary aside, you're the most obedient, conscientious, straight-laced person I've ever met. It had to be some stupid asinine rule that no one but your medieval father would care about. You know what your problem is? You didn't tell your parents to get stuffed enough growing up. If you disappoint them consistently, regularly, and in ever-increasing orders of magnitude, you'd have to be guilty of murder to get them to bat an eyelash. Trust me, I'm living proof."

And, like magic, the guilty weight lifted from her shoulders. Part of her had always believed her parents' unrealistic expectations bore a significant portion of the blame for their estrangement, but to have it articulated by someone she cared about brought unexpected relief. "Well, it's too late for me to follow in your footsteps. By the way, you missed the turn to my side of town."

He snorted. "Sweetheart, this car is not going anywhere near Capital South. You're staying at my place."

Her breath didn't quite make it to her lungs. While she could stare down criminals and keep her fear in check, the thought of spending the night with Jack triggered her flight-or-fight response. Logic commanded she put her foot down and insist he drop her off at the nearest Metro stop. But then she remembered him enveloping her in those strong arms, how the mere scent of him had driven away all traces of terror. Though any more time together might upturn their precarious balance, she couldn't stand being home alone. "I'll go stay with some friends. You can drop me off—"

"Do those friends of yours live somewhere with round-the-clock security? What about an alarm system? Those thugs must have followed you from your place—if they've been watching you, they might know who you hang out with."

She had a sinking suspicion there might be a grain of truth to his argument. Sweets had stayed with her all afternoon, and they'd walked to the Metro together. If not for her friend's presence, the attack might have occurred much sooner. With the situation escalated, she wasn't so sure going to her pal's place would be the best of ideas. "I handled the situation, didn't I?"

"Like you handled the break-ins?" The sneaky little eavesdropper sounded far too smug. "While we're on the subject, owning hideous cheap shit is not a solution for a recurring burglar. You should have called the cops."

He must have been listening in for quite some time. "And send my brother to prison?"

"He'll end up there soon enough." They turned into the underground parking garage of a Georgetown condo building. "And your dad's not as dumb as you think. He must have cut off your brother's funds if Tony bothered robbing you."

She'd come to a similar conclusion. Her father was too proud to apologize, but in the spirit of Christmas, she might give him a call tomorrow. They pulled up right in front of the elevator bank. The location had plenty of clearance on either side. "Wow. This is a prime parking spot."

"One of the perks of owning the penthouse. Come up and check out the view, at least. We can discuss the rest of the night over some drinks—or Perrier, in your case. A glass of wine on an empty stomach might knock you out cold."

Curiosity got the better of her. She wanted to see where he lived, what he'd done to make this place his home. Intuition told her something had changed between them when he wrapped his arms around her tonight—something she might not be ready for. But he'd reverted to his usual self, so what was the harm?

Stepping out, she grabbed her coat and hung it over one arm. "How can you afford this place on a junior associate's salary?" The attorneys made a decent amount, but nothing that'd pay for Italian sports cars and luxury condos. Frost Senior had a reputation for stinginess.

Grabbing his briefcase, Jack walked to her side. By the time he reached her, the doors had shut. "I came into my trust fund six years ago. I descend from a long line of ancestors who liked making money more than spending it. I'm the black sheep."

She followed him into a private glass elevator. As the numbers on the digital screen increased, he placed an arm around her shoulder. Detecting an undercurrent of anxiety, she turned to face him. "What's wrong?"

He shrugged. "You're my first houseguest. I should warn you—I haven't had much time to go furniture shopping."

Chapter Five

Stepping through the thick doors into the dark, freezing foyer, Mina struggled to fill her lungs. Bouncing from foot to foot, she rubbed her hands over her upper arms and tried to stay warm. The low temperature inside the dimly lit apartment rivaled the chill outside. Taking her coat, Jack marched past her and turned on a light. What she saw rooted her to the spot. "Oh hell."

He hooked her garment on a hatstand created out of ice. His briefcase landed on the small table beside it—a polished cube of frozen water the size of large suitcase. He pulled off his shoes and socks, placing them in a cubby carved into the entryway wall.

Ignoring her, he padded to the center of the penthouse to stand by a giant pillar comparable in size to a large closet. A moment later, the gas fireplace within it blazed to life. Encased in a clear gleaming column, the dancing orange flames reflected off the various translucent creations in his home.

Responding to the black remote in his hand, more overhead lights turned on, bathing the penthouse in an eerie white glow. Acting on autopilot, she peeled off her boots, her gaze flitting back and forth to take in one marvel after the other.

In stocking feet, she inched forward over the frigid expanse to join him on the white sheepskin rug in front of the fire. By the time she got there, she thought her toes might freeze off. The floors were covered in a thick layer of ice but dusted with powdery snow to minimize slippage. Every single piece of furniture she could see seemed conjured from a combination of the two forms of solidified liquid.

Standing by the flames, she had an unimpeded view of the kitchen area. Aside from the appliances, he'd encased every inch of the expansive space in frost. Huge blocks of ice formed the countertops and island, with transparent cylindrical trunks serving as stools. Closer to where they stood, a rectangular glacier acted as his dining table. Hollowed balls of packed snow surrounded it like a phalanx of egg-shaped chairs.

Boxy ice sofas bordered the rug they stood on, their seats covered in the same white sheepskin. On the other side of the fireplace, open internal doors framed a frozen slab the size of a king-sized bed, which was topped with a thin mattress pad and two pillows, all encased in smooth ivory sheets.

She cleared her throat. "Okay, well this has been fun. Before I touch something and get frostbite, I'm going to go...."

"Don't be such a scaredy cat." He grabbed her wrist and pressed the back of her hand against the wall next to the hearth. To her surprise, it felt cool, but not freezing. "I figured out a way to fluctuate energy levels so the surfaces warm on skin contact. If you take off those tights, your little toes won't be as cold."

Stunned by the extent of his control, she freed her hand so she could trail it over the ornate glacial mantelpiece where two white-eyed dragons faced each other at the pinnacle of the fire. Though flames blazed within, the giant smooth pillar showed no signs of melting. "So you're the Ice Maestro."

Placing the remote by her unsteady fingers, he splayed one hand over her nape before bending down to brush his lips against her cheek. A sense of rightness seeped through his hold, along with staggering certainty and the rush of possession. His chest warmed her back, his free arm snaking around her torso. His fingers gripping her waist, he turned her to face him.

The flames lent his angular face an eerie luminescence. In a black shirt and charcoal suit, surrounded by evidence of the power he wielded, he'd never appeared more dangerous. But he was still Jack—her Jack. And she could never be afraid of him.

Guiding her to the chilly surface beside the fire, he crowded her until she flattened her back against the pillar of ice. She marveled at the dichotomy—her bare arms and neck were comfortably cool, while her torso came close to freezing under the silk. His hand still at her neck, he bent down to nip her earlobe. "Did you like my Godzilla? I didn't get to see your reaction."

The barrage of arousal pouring through the contact threatened her already precarious balance. Too confused by the sudden change in his demeanor, she kept her tone casual. "Please tell me you didn't make those sculptures to see how I'd react?"

He tugged down her collar and kissed her neck. "Not the first one. I needed an outlet, and the Datagate scandal was all over the news. But then I heard you laugh when you saw the photo. I liked the sound." He pressed his teeth against the sensitive skin below her ear. His tongue pulsed over the spot before he sucked.

Moaning, she threw her head back against the glacial wall. Deep down, she understood what his words meant—what the simple act of showing her his home meant—even if the truth hadn't yet occurred to him.

Needing time to think and room to breathe, she pushed at his chest. "Back off for a sec. Why did you insist you didn't have any magic?"

Giving her two more inches of space, he loosened his tie. The platinum clip landed on the white fur, the diamond twinkling to catch her eye. Ignoring the accessory, he pulled the loop over his head and tossed it over his shoulder. "I was about to leave for Boston. My father wrote a contract for your parents to sign. He wanted to send you with me as my pet kitten for the low price of your brother's bail."

She bit her lower lip. "So you rejected magic for me?"

He shrugged out of his suit jacket and threw it to the side. "I try not to overthink things. I told Dad to fuck off because it felt good. That's all there was to it."

When he lifted his wrist and canted his head, she reached for his cuff and fumbled with the link. Making sure not to touch him, she used the reprieve to sift through her own emotions. She'd always wanted this, but not now, not yet. Anything she started with him wouldn't be skin deep. This wasn't a meaningless hook-up—a night of sex ending in a good-bye kiss and vague plans they'd never keep.

He wasn't thinking straight, hadn't been since she ran into him tonight. With quintessential male arrogance, he seemed focused on the present, acting on a desire so intense it threatened to overwhelm her. She'd come into contact with arousal before, but not from someone she also wanted. Her brief experimentation with sex had been the product of curiosity, an academic endeavor.

But with Jack, the primitive indefinable urge was mirrored within her, the slow, relentless burn reflecting, echoing, and amplifying until she feared she might go mad. She couldn't suppress the raging need to have his breath against her pulse, his palms on her skin. Her fingertips itched to learn the texture of his five o'clock shadow; her lips throbbed in an invitation for him to bite and taste.

She'd thought these desires the product of her empathy and his urges, but this brief moment of respite opened her eyes. He might be brimming with cold fire, but the molten heat driving her to the precipice had come from a part of her she hadn't known existed. This wasn't a youth's hero worship or a teenager's infatuation. She wanted him with a hunger she feared might never be sated.

When she managed to get the damn cufflink off, he lifted his other wrist. Repeating the process with surer fingers, she kept her eyes glued to his chest. When she had both sets in one hand, she took a deep breath, met his silver gaze, and turned her palm down to let the metal chips fall.

Jack reached over Mina's head and tugged out the metal pins. As he placed them on the mantle beside her, one by one, he filled his lungs with the scent of cinnamon and cloves floating off her hair.

She sighed. "You have no idea what I went through for that up-do."

"I never liked it when you tied your hair." A few more pulls dislodged the coiled bun. The braid unwound into a long queue that reached her ribcage. Placing one hand above her head on the pillar, he reached around her waist and tugged the elastic free.

She stepped toward him, her head tilting up. Their breaths mingled, her midnight eyes hooded by a dark fan of lowered lashes. "You never seemed to give a damn about how I looked."

"For an empath, you're not much good at reading minds. I almost grabbed you by the ponytail one day with every intention of freezing off the godawful scrunchie. Those things went out of style in the nineties." She remained motionless as he worked his fingers through the silken strands, unraveling the thick mane until it fanned over her back and surrounded her delicate shoulders. He wanted to see her like this, without a single stitch on her. "There. Much better."

Her brows furrowed. "You never considered kissing me before. What changed?"

Hell if he knew. Ever since he'd watched those bastards drag her away, he'd been faced with several unsettling realizations. He needed her in his home where he could keep her safe, and he would launch the next Ice Age to achieve that goal. Having the right to hold her whenever he pleased, to touch her wherever he desired, superseded all of his other priorities. To top off the series of odd revelations, he wanted her to run into his arms the way she had tonight at least once a day—no, more often than that.

Trying to find a single cohesive explanation for all the caveman-like urges that had bubbled to the fore in the past thirty minutes gave him a headache, so he resolved not to give it any more thought. He'd much rather act out every compulsion that came to mind.

He'd always been fascinated by her skin—pale and snowy white, but worlds apart from his own, the texture finer, smoother, and interlaced with hints of gold. So he brushed his lips over her lowered eyelids, trailed them down her small nose, and slid them over her soft, round cheeks. His tongue lashed out to tease the corner of her mouth, capitalized on her quick intake of breath to push inside.

He tasted her, the hesitant reciprocal tangling not enough to take even the slightest edge off his hunger. Circling her neck with both hands, he held her captive and took control of the sensuous dance. Later, much later, he might regain the patience to take things slow and easy.

When she sagged against his chest, he broke the kiss. "What am I feeling?"

He needed her to tell him. He couldn't explain the pounding in his ears or the electric heat coating his skin. Her swollen lips incited a hunger he didn't understand—a visceral need to claim more than her body, to keep her with him long after tonight.

Her lashes hovered over her pale cheeks. Then her lids lifted to reveal those chocolate eyes. Beneath the glaze of arousal, he detected a hint of trepidation. "Confusion, euphoria, possession, desire, and a dozen other things."

All the words fit, but their combination eluded comprehension. Focusing on the most potent impulse, he slid one hand under the hem of her short crimson dress and ran his palm up her thigh. "This might get a little cold."

Protecting her skin with a thin layer of pure energy, he froze the tights so fast they disintegrated into powdery ice. Gasping, she grabbed the sides of his upper arms, her slender fingers clinging to his shirt. "My panties...."

He'd gotten rid of those, too. "Oops."

His erection strained against tented trousers, his cock so hard the zipper dug into the ridge. Deciding to give her a taste of his discomfort, he wedged his knee between her legs. Pushing her against the wall, he grabbed her butt and lifted, positioning his crotch over the crimson silk that had bunched up to form an inadequate layer of protection. Her hands lifted to his shoulders, her grasp tightening as he ground into her.

She gasped, her lids fluttering each time he pumped his hips. After watching the way she reacted to the indirect stimulation, he couldn't wait to fuck her. But, first, he needed to see her naked.

Deciding to keep her in this vulnerable position, he conjured a slab of ice to form a ledge under her ass. She yelped, her eyes growing wide as he smoothed his palms up her front and yanked at the fabric buttons under her collar. "I like this dress. I'd rather leave it in one piece."

His hands on her chest, he could feel the erratic rise and fall of her every breath. "There's...there's a back zipper."

That mystery solved, he trailed fingers over the patterned scarlet-and-gold surface. With his thumb, he traced the shape of a puckered nipple. "You're not wearing a bra."

Her cheeks turned a deeper red. "The dress doesn't leave enough room."

The painted-on garment had driven him crazy ever since she first got into his car. Managing to drive home without crashing was a minor miracle. The moment she took off her coat, he'd wanted to explore her subtle curves, to rend the silk to shreds and spread her thighs.

Closing a hand over her breast, he squeezed. When her mouth parted, he took possession. Melting away the ledge's edge until a few inches remained, he caught her waist and held her in place. He matched his tongue's rhythm to the shifting of his hips, grinding into her as he plundered. Trembling, she arched her back and clung to his shoulders. With a surrendering moan, her teeth scraped over his lower lip, a softer, more hesitant version of the caress he'd inflicted mere moments ago.

The kiss dragged on in an unrelenting crescendo. She yanked his shirt out of the waistband and ran her hands up his back. The slide of skin against skin sent an electric jolt to his cock, her fevered exploration turning his zipper into an instrument of torture. He retaliated by sucking her tongue into his mouth, by tormenting her lower lip while milking her breasts with both hands. Her roaming fingers jerked, closing to form fists against his shoulder blades.

The inferno inside him demanding more, he inserted one hand between her and the ice, running his palm up her spine until he reached the clasp at the collar. In a single, smooth move, he pulled the zipper down to her lower back.

When he grabbed the parted silk and tried to yank it off her shoulders, she broke the kiss and pushed him back. Panting, she leaned against the ice and moved one hand to clutch the dress to her chest. Her eyes glued to his face, she slid her free arm out of the sleeve before mirroring the motion on the other side. Holding the fabric in place, she canted her head. "You first."

He took a step back to take in the view. Her legs bared and spread, with a swath of crimson obscuring her front, she presented an erotic picture against the glittering ice. The flames at their side danced off her almost-naked form. Creamy skin contrasted with her ebony hair, its subtle golden hints highlighted by the flickering yellow-and-orange light. If he didn't get to see the body under that dress soon, he'd go insane.

He stepped closer, pressing into her once more. "Give me a hand."

A mischievous grin dimpling her cheeks, she batted her eyelashes. Without her moving a muscle, his buttons came undone, one after the other. When his shirt parted, he shook his head and lowered his arms. "Cheater."

"You're the one who's freezing me to death. The wall isn't icy, but the air's still cold." The starched cotton slid over his shoulders, down his limbs, and fell to the floor. "Want me to drop your pants, too?"

He lifted an eyebrow in challenge. "Go ahead." After the stunt she'd pulled earlier tonight, he doubted she had much more magic up her sleeve.

After her next attempt at telekinesis resulted in no more than a slight vibration around his hips, she huffed out a breath.

Keeping her left hand over her chest, she wrestled his belt buckle with her right. After some halfhearted yanking resulted in nothing more than his growing erection, he grabbed the darn thing and undid it. Groaning with relief as the trousers' fastenings came apart, he shoved his pants down along with his underwear.

Kicking them off his feet, he rose to see her balancing on the ledge, her back plastered to the wall. "Why are you making a weird face?"

She licked her lips. "You're bigger than...than I expected."

He turned to give her a profile view. "Have you heard the saying, 'it's not the size, it's how you use it'?"

She bit her lip but failed to suppress a laugh. "Maybe."

Facing her, he closed the distance between them. "It's a load of bull."

She chortled and wobbled on the edge. Extending both arms, she braced her weight on his chest. The dress fell to circle her waist. Trepidation replaced some of the mirth in her eyes as she stared up at him.

Though he'd gotten the briefest glimpse, the flash of delicate curves sent more blood pooling to his groin. From this angle, he had an unimpeded view of her back—an expanse of smooth flesh leading to a tiny waist and rounded bottom. Her nipples brushed his skin, her breasts soft against his much-harder chest.

Her lips parted, her eyes widening as her shoulders sagged. She blew out a breath.

He shook his head, marveling at how clueless she could be. "You're so beautiful, I can't think straight."

The corners of her mouth curved up. "You're telling the truth."

"Of course I am." He pushed her shoulders back against the ice. "Stay still and let me look at you."

He cupped her breasts, weighing them with his hands. Though shy of filling his palms, the pert globes appeared lush against her delicate frame. Rosy nipples tipped off the porcelain perfection, begging to be pinched and sucked. His gaze dropped to her belly, his fingers tracing the shadowed grooves of muscle accentuated by the firelight. He followed the shifting lines past her navel to the smooth triangle between her legs. When he slid his thumb over her slit, slippery wetness coated his skin.

"Jack...."

Plumping her left breast with one hand, he lowered his head and closed his mouth over the tip. She whimpered and pushed at his shoulders, her spine arching and her butt scooting back. Trapped between him and a glacial wall, she had nowhere to run. As his tongue circled, he breached her with a finger, invading her tight channel.

Soft cries echoed around him. He scraped his teeth over the pink bud before biting lightly down. Her hands clamped around his head, pulling him into her chest as her hips shifted toward his invasion. Distracting her with a hard suck, he pushed a second digit into her.

"Fuck...." Her fingers curled around his hair before her arms dropped to her sides.

Feeling her muscles tense, he pulled out by a fraction. Relinquishing her breast, he lifted his head so he could see her face. "I didn't peg you for the dirty-talking type."

She'd squeezed her eyes shut. "And you talk too much."

Considering his options, he used his thumb to part her labia before pressing the pad over her clit. When he circled, her eyes popped open. Chuckling, he asked, "Really?"

She glared at him. Shallow gasps punctuated her words. "Don't... sound... so... smug."

He continued to stimulate her, his mouth curving when her hands fisted. With her distracted, he spread his fingers and pumped them in and out, readying her for the next item on his agenda. "Any chance you're on the pill?"

Moaning, she shook her head.

It'd been worth a shot. "Okay, well, think about how you can get a condom over here while I do this."

Kneeling between her legs, he removed his thumb and replaced it with his mouth.

"Wait...." She grabbed his shoulders, her fingernails digging into his deltoids. Sucking her clit, he swirled his tongue around it, burying his fingers deep inside her in the same instant. She tried to close her legs. Her knees clamped over his upper arms.

He countered her futile resistance by blowing a gust of frigid air over her clit, warming it an instant later with his tongue. She whimpered. "Oh God...I'm about to...." Quickening his penetration, he switched between hot and cold until she screamed, her inner muscles clamping in a flurry around his fingers.

Wiping his mouth, he freed his hand and glanced up to find her eyes closed, her skin pink and covered in sweat. A circle of purple foil packets on the floor caught his eye. The crafty little witch must have teleported them over while he'd been busy making her come.

He grabbed the closest condom and stood. Reading the label, he shook his head. Only a woman would buy the ultra-thin maximum sensations variety.

Her heavy lids had lifted by the time he finished smoothing on the latex. He gestured at the extra protection on floor with a tilt of his head. "You think we have enough?"

Her breaths still shallow, her eyes widened. Then one corner of her mouth lifted. "That depends on your performance."

Grabbing her waist, he positioned his cock against her slick opening. "I'm an exceed-expectations kind of guy."

Pulling his head down, she bit his lower lip. "Oh yeah?"

"Always."

Sealing her mouth with his own, he held her in place and pushed forward, laying claim on her inch by torturous inch. She was tight as a fist. Breaking the kiss, he slid his hands under her ass, bracing her weight as he willed away the icy ledge that had kept her in position. When she wrapped her arms around his shoulders, he relaxed his muscles and allowed gravity to bring her down, impaling her on his cock until he was buried to the hilt.

He groaned. "You have no idea how good this feels."

Resting her head in the crook of his neck, she whispered into his ear, "Empath, remember?" Then she clenched her inner muscles, squeezing his length and nearly sending him over the edge.

He stepped backward until his calf met a covered block of ice. A dozen unvoiced expletives racing through his head, he bent his knees and sat on the white fur. "Move."

Her hands on his shoulders, she straddled him, her knees on either side of his thighs. In a slow, sinuous shift, she lifted her bottom until only the tip of his shaft was surrounded in damp heat. "Or what?"

Placing the pad of his thumb over her clit, he sent through a low hum of energy—enough for a chilled vibration. She clawed his delts, her breath turning shallow once more. When he moved his hand down, her hips followed it. He rewarded the maddening shimmy with another pulse. "You can take more of me than that."

When she didn't respond fast enough, he grabbed her waist with both hands and yanked her down. She gasped as he filled her, her small body writhing on his lap. Inserting his fingers once more between them, he circled the bundle of nerves. He hadn't heard her scream enough.

Her eyes hooding at the direct stimulation, she bent her head forward, her long hair falling to brush his abs. The cascade of silk framed her torso, drawing his attention to her chest. Lifting his free arm, he circled her breast's coral tip with his index finger, leaving behind a thin ring of ice. Her back arched. Her hips shifted forward.

Her slick channel slid down his length, the friction an exquisite torture. As a reward, he treated her other breast to the same magic, the cold clamp forcing both to erect attention. He laved the first nipple with his tongue, circled until all the frost melted. His fingers danced over her clit, drawing her forward and back, luring her to ride him. Her inexperience showed—her rhythm too erratic, her impalement too shallow and languid to satisfy his needs. But fighting not to come had never been this close to impossible.

He switched to her other breast, his tongue drawing high-pitched cries from her throat. When she dug her fingernails into her skin, he flicked his thumb and sent her once more over the precipice. Her orgasm milked his cock, the relaxing and tensing of muscles a symphony of exquisite pleasure and torture. His control snapping, he grabbed her thighs and stood.

Spinning in place, tumbled her back on the fur-covered ice. He pumped his hips, savoring her moans as he drove into her in an unrelenting rhythm. Her arms and legs tightened around him, her breasts flattening against his chest. She bit his shoulder, her screams muffled as he took her hard and fast.

Each thrust layered another wave of pleasure, the friction building until the cascade approached pain. His perception narrowed to only encompass the woman in his arms—the scent of musk and spice, the feel of sweat-slicked skin and soft pliant flesh. His vision turned red, his cock threatening to explode.

Cold fire bloomed behind his closed lids. She spasmed, her entire body tensing as she threw her head back and moaned his name. Surrendering to the blaze, he hurtled them into oblivion.

Chapter Six

*A*s Jack began to lose circulation in his left arm, he glanced around his glacial penthouse and came to a decision. He needed to buy some actual furniture. When he'd moved in, the prospect of picking shit out and having it delivered hadn't appealed. So he'd conjured what he needed as the days went by and, a week later, ended up with an apartment covered in ice.

Since he'd never planned to bring anyone home, he hadn't cared too much about normalcy. The temperature in here suited him to perfection, but Mina came from much less sturdy stock. The surfaces might warm on touch, but the massive amount of ice chilled the air. She couldn't venture more than a few feet away from the fireplace without her teeth chattering. By the time she trekked over to the master bathroom, she'd gotten so cold she'd decided to draw a bath. When he went searching for her, it led to some interesting new uses for the air jets.

But the tub got tepid real quick, due in part to the fact that he'd encased it in a miniature glacier. So they ended up back where they started, with her small form engulfed in one of his dress shirts, curled up on the rug.

Maybe he should add blankets to the shopping list. He'd never needed them, but he could see why a few might come in handy. While he had very fond memories of the twelve or so square feet they occupied, staying there didn't seem like a long-term solution without additional sources of warmth.

Not that he was sure this thing with her was heading anywhere, or anything crazy like that. But it didn't hurt to make plans for the weekend, or the next couple of weeks, or hell, maybe even the next few months.

He poked her shoulder with his index finger. "Are you done sleeping yet?"

"No." She growled. "It's been fifteen minutes."

Closer to twenty, but who was counting? "They teach poor children in D.C., too, by the way."

Without lifting her lids, she reached over and covered his mouth. "Shh...."

He lifted her wrist and moved her arm to his waist. How could she ignore him when they had something important to discuss? "Did you hear what I said?"

"If you *ever* want to have sex again, you'll shut up."

He rolled his eyes at the empty threat. She'd enjoyed it at least as much as he had. Besides, after capping off round three in the bath, even *his* penis needed a break. "I said you don't need to move to stupid Detroit for that program. I googled it. They do the same stuff here, too."

She pinched his abs. "I already know. Shush."

He rubbed the spot. The injury warranted retaliation. With a smirk, he moved his left arm out from under her face.

Her eyes snapped open. "I'm going to kill you."

Lying on his side, he propped his head up on one elbow. "Then who'll get you strawberries and chocolate fondue in ten minutes?"

The promise seemed to mollify her. She mirrored his position and grabbed his hand. "Teach for America was a *way* for me to move. My life here has gotten difficult."

"Because of your thieving brother, who's since skipped town."

She sighed. "Which has created even more problems."

He grunted. "I'm pretty sure those gangsters learned their lesson. If not, there's this organization called the police, which you can contact by dialing 9-1-1. If all else fails, I'll freeze off sections of Chinatown. Any other excuses for leaving?"

"Besides not having a reason to stay?"

"What am I, chopped liver?" When she lifted her eyebrows and responded with slow blink, he cleared his throat. "We're friends, aren't we?"

She drummed her fingers on his knuckles but said nothing. He hated it when she used silence as a form of psychological warfare. It had something to do with it always working.

"We're...like...closer friends than normal." A chill skittered down his spine as he said the words.

Judging from the half-dimples on her cheeks, he suspected she suppressed a smile. He could feel beads of moisture form on his forehead. He *never* sweated. "I consider you...my best bud since Leo's gone AWOL."

She bit her lower lip, which continued to quiver despite the clamping row of neat white teeth.

"And I want us to hang out together more, maybe do dinner...and lunch...and breakfast...which we can't do, if you're in another state."

She batted her eyelashes. "No sex?"

"Of course, sex." The possibility of jeopardizing that threatened to give him a panic attack. "Lots of sex."

"I see." She drew circles on the back of his hand. "Should we still also try to have sex with other people?"

He resisted the urge to massage his throat, which had turned into the Sahara. "You might not want to, you know. After you've got a taste of the primo stuff, other dudes won't cut it."

The throaty sound she made was somewhere between a cough and a laugh. "And you?"

He shuddered. "Do you have any idea how much money and effort goes into getting laid? Why would I go through the trouble if I can get much better sex from you for free?"

She shook her head and looked up at the ceiling. "You have a way with words, you know that?"

Detecting sarcasm, he admitted defeat and switched tactics.

He'd always been better at showing than telling. With a wave of his hand, a small storm formed above them, the ice crystals coalescing until a thick, solid, glacial trunk grew to twice his height. Grabbing her by the waist, he rolled them until she lay nestled against his chest, her face turned up to watch the magic.

Smoothing his hand over her hair, he added individual needles and pinecones. Once an entire tree floated in the air, he lowered it a few feet away from their heads so the bottommost branch hovered mere inches above their faces.

She brushed the intricate network of frost with her fingertips. "Wow."

He pressed a kiss to her cheek. "Spend Christmas with me."

She turned and perched on his chest. As she stared into his eyes, her dark hair fell to curtain the sides of her face. Spreading his fingers over on the back of her neck, he pulled her down so he could capture her lips. When the slow, sipping kiss ended, she smiled and rested her forehead on his. "Just this one?"

He slid his hands under her shirt and circled her waist, allowing her to sense what he wasn't yet ready to admit. "No. Not just this one."

FIREWORKS AT MIDNIGHT

Chapter One

*D*ulcina Gato hated few things more than going through the day without coffee.

After she got her high school diploma and landed a minimum-wage job, she rode the independence high and turned down her parents' allowance. When she made the mistake of spending her precious paychecks on a bachelor's degree, she downgraded from Starbucks flavored lattes to less-than-adequate espresso shots. After spending years in online and night classes to earn a piece of paper that hadn't increased her income by a single cent, she went on a descending spiral past donut-store drip to land at the bottom of the caffeine rabbit hole, fast-food chain budget brews. Even this luxury went the way of the dodo when she had the bright idea of quitting her dead-end day job to turn her jewelry-making hobby into a small business.

The ten-dollar coffee maker she'd bought at a flea market had long since died a slow and torturous death, and all she had left to keep her going at 7:00 a.m. on New Year's Eve was an instant cup of Joe. She stared at her orange mug through the grease-stained translucent door of the circa-1980s microwave, wondering why it took so long to heat up water. As soon as she got her hands on the money Flowers Forever had raked in over the Christmas shopping season, she'd invest in one of those electric kettles.

Her vision hazed. Through fluttering lashes, an overlay of smoke and flames flashed over the worn laminate counter. Starting from behind the appliance, a black smear snaked up the peeling wallpaper to reach the dirt-encrusted popcorn ceiling.

Shaking her head to dispel the burst of foresight, she yawned. *Shit. How fucking inconvenient.* She glanced down at her torso, too sleepy to remember what she'd pulled on last night when she got out of the shower. Bright-blue nighttime shorts and a matching tank top might not be ideal for greeting a cavalry of firemen. Washington, D.C.'s prolonged arctic winter had turned her once-tanned skin a sallow yellow, which acquired a sickly sheen when paired with her clothes' clashing aqua. Considering she'd scheduled her next beach vacation in ten years, she needed to avoid cold hues for the foreseeable future.

If push came to shove, she should have enough time to pull on something more flattering and run a brush through her hair. Upsides of the shoulder-length schoolgirl bob included the ten-dollar price tag and extreme low maintenance. Since highlights grew out faster than she could save up money, she eschewed artificial color in favor of her natural drab brown. She hadn't been born with her sister's brains, and lack of scholarships meant she came out of the undergraduate rip-off with a mountain of student loans.

Growing up had turned out to be a huge bummer. The year's end came with an insane amount of incidental expenses for the fledgling company she'd started with Shelley Dupree, her best friend since pre-kindergarten. While she and her business partner could legally buy alcohol at long last, affording any seemed out of their reach. Paying next year's fee for their website, which she'd put off until the previous evening, had almost netted them bank overdraft fees. No way could they get a new microwave in the foreseeable future.

"Shells," she bellowed. "The kitchen is about to catch on fire."

Her short-legged pal bounded in less than a minute later. Wearing a pink sweatshirt and matching pajama bottoms, the petite twenty-one-year-old earth mage could pass for a high schooler. Leaves and flower petals dusted her chestnut hair; dirt smudged her flushed café au lait cheeks. "Sweets, I swear to God—if this is your idea of a joke, I'll bury you."

Dulcina preferred the nickname Sweets to the name her parents had bestowed upon her in an unfortunate moment of nostalgia—the single reason she could come up with to explain why both she and her sister had such distinctly Spanish names. And while her sibling's Catalina got shortened to a neutral Cat, Sweets' legal name always ended up as some permutation of Douche, Dull-Chai, or China. "Why are *you* so grumpy?"

Shelley placed her hands on the lush hips Sweets had been green-eyed about since they'd turned thirteen. "I'm in the middle of harvesting blooms. If we leave them out too long, they'll be useless."

As always, Shelley had woken before dawn to mess around in the greenhouse they maintained in the backyard. The tropical flowers the witch's elemental powers kept alive would soon be dried, coated in several layers of resin, and fitted with silver findings. Once done, they sold the jewelry online and at their stall in the Sunday market in Georgetown.

Though they both loved the work, the start-up phase came with more expenses than profit. Placing one elbow on the peeling counter, Sweets stared at the coffee she'd never drink. "I saw it happen. This piece of crap is going to fry."

Few people knew about her foresight. To help keep it a secret, Shelley accepted attribution for all premonitions they disclosed. Her ancient supernatural bloodline made the emergence of a weak secondary power plausible, and her privileged status as an elemental witch allowed her to keep the Mage's Council at arm's length. "Well this sucks. How long do we have?"

"You know how short the fuse is on visions. Plain old vibes gives us a few days, but when I see things happen in Technicolor, the goose is almost cooked."

Moving closer and bending down to squint at the old

appliance, Shelley suggested, "Should we turn it off? Unplug it and stuff?"

Sweets canted her head. "If it's an electrical thing, wouldn't touching it zap us?" She looked down at her bare feet. "So being 'grounded'?" She used her fingers to form air quotes. "Is that when you're wearing shoes or not wearing shoes?"

Scrunching her nose, Shelley shrugged. "I don't know. And are we supposed to *be* grounded before we touch the outlet, or the other away round?"

Sweets narrowed her eyes at the humming hunk of metal. "How can you not know this, Ms. Smarty-Pants? You've got a science degree." At times, she questioned the veracity of their standardized test scores. According to the numbers, Shelley had scored a tenth of a percentile below genius while Sweets fell smack dab in the lower half of average.

"In *biology*, not electrical engineering." Shelley sniffed the air. "I smell something burning."

Sweets filled her lungs. "Me, too. It should have pinged already, and the dial isn't turning."

"Can't you unplug it with your mind, or, I don't know, dematerialize it?" An elemental mage, Shelley had the ability to control one thing—the earth. They both agreed this might be the most useless form of magic imaginable. As her friend's familiar, Sweets could process that raw energy and turn it into more useful spells, including telekinesis, teleportation, illusion, and enchantments. Since she hadn't applied herself much to the study of magic, her actual abilities didn't extend far beyond moving stuff around with her mind.

One minor problem prevented the plug's safe evacuation. "I'm out of juice. I haven't turned into a cat in two weeks."

"Well, the visions haven't stopped. Didn't I tell you going cold turkey would bite us in the ass?" Shelley loved few things in life more than saying, *I told you so.*

Foreseeing bad shit came hand in hand with the compulsion to do something about it. While Sweets had managed to wiggle out of each sticky situation, she didn't want to push her luck. She processed leaked power best by assuming her familiar form. Since she and Shelley didn't have the most compatible energy profiles, they shared little magic while she stayed human. As an experiment, she'd sworn off her feline persona in hopes that the premonitions would cease. But while every single other ability petered into nonexistence, the one she wanted to purge continued to plague her day and night.

She huffed out a breath and admitted defeat. "Fine. Hold on." With a pop, she turned into a plain coffee-colored cat. None of the good genes had been left by the time she came around. Not only did she have nondescript brown hair and eyes, a body with more angles than curves, and a rare power that painted a giant red bull's-eye on her back, her animal alter ego couldn't be less memorable.

As soon as sleek silky fur covered her skin, raw energy poured into her—more than she'd expected. If she didn't know better, she'd have guessed another elemental mage was close by, one who shared more synergy with her than Shelley. The charge built at an exponential rate. A few more seconds and—

Flames erupted from the back of the microwave. Scampering to hide behind her friend's legs, she focused on the burning metal box and lifted it into the air. The power cord swept forward, upending the canisters lining the wall. Digging her claws into linoleum, she yanked the plug out of the socket with a telekinetic pull.

Suspended in the middle of the kitchen where the fire couldn't spread to the walls or ceiling, the old appliance continued to release a steady stream of pungent black smoke. Loud, high-pitched beeps filled the small room and threatened to burst Sweets' oversensitive feline eardrums. Needing to concentrate on keeping the darn thing up, she swatted Shelley's ankle with her tail in an attempt to urge the witch into action. Talk about being useless in a crisis.

Shelley looked down at her. "Where's the fire extinguisher?"

Come to think of it, that particular item might have fallen under the useful-but-not-necessary category when she came up with their list of things to buy. Pawing her face in shame, she meowed. Witches and familiars communicated on a cerebral level somewhere between telepathy and miming.

"I thought so." Covering her mouth with an arm, Shelley began to cough. "Let me think. What are the chances that thing is all metal?"

Sweets turned her head from side to side in the most emphatic no she could achieve as a cat. In theory, Shelley should control all solids originating from the ground, which included plants, minerals, sand, and therefore their metal and glass derivatives. Petroleum fell into a gray area in the elemental Venn diagram between earth and fire, and the presence of plastic in any item messed up Shelley's already unpredictable mojo. While the witch's powers gave her a supernaturally green thumb, her actual ability to manipulate metal seemed to miss more often than it hit, leading time and again to catastrophic consequences.

Sweets lifted her front paw to shield her eyes while meowing an inarticulate plea. Ignoring the protest, her friend squared her shoulders and raised her hands. As she wiggled her fingers in a weird, creepy pattern, the rectangular box crumpled to form a ball, closing the flames within. Smoke continued to puff out, but the fire soon smoldered.

Okay, perhaps the witch deserved more credit. Before the notion took root, the ball exploded, sending shrapnel in all directions. Hissing, Sweets halted their progress with a telekinetic blast, freezing them in the air a split second before sharp metal hit her friend's face. Using more magic than she thought she possessed, she forced the shards to drift to the floor.

Her lungs burning, she shifted back to human form. Pointing to the back entrance, she hacked, "Need. Air. Move."

Wearing a guilty expression, Shelley blocked her ears with her hands and ran to open the door, her fluffy slippers making squishy sounds as she covered the distance. "Where's the smoke detector?"

Sweets slumped onto the linoleum floor with a tired groan. Magic was draining work. "This is *your* grandmother's old house."

She flopped onto her back and closed her eyes. When her head started to pound from the continuing squeals, she drew a fortifying breath and tried to summon the energy to get up. Before she gathered enough motivation, a gust of wind blew through the kitchen, pushing the thick, pungent smoke outside. By the time her eyes stopped watering, sweet-smelling, pristine air filled the small room. Aside from the scorched metallic mess, all signs of smoke dissipated.

She didn't need visual confirmation to be certain which wind mage had reconditioned the environs and provided the source of her extra energy. Forcing her lids open, she met the dark, judgmental gaze of a familiar mahogany-skinned warlock. Standing by the kitchen entrance with his head grazing the sill, Mikal Knight lifted his long arm to pound at a piece of round white plastic above the wood frame. A few seconds later, the electronic wail stopped.

His gruff, masculine voice soon interrupted the brief, blissful silence. "Good morning, brats. Celebrating New Year's Eve with some fireworks, I see." No one had the right to sound this upbeat at a quarter past seven, not even him.

"Midnight. Oh, my gosh!" With a headache-intensifying squeal, Shelley leapt across the room to wrap her arms around her older half-brother. "What are you doing here? I thought you couldn't take time off work."

Letting her head fall to the rubbery tile, Sweets stared at the disintegrating ceiling and contemplated turning back into a cat. The last thing she wanted right this second was a chat with the walking Armani advertisement. What was he doing in an open-collar white shirt and dark-blue suit at this time of day?

She could smell his spicy cologne from where she slumped, and his short beard was trimmed to ruler-straight lines alongside his mouth and under his dimpled chin. Of course he'd show up looking like a GQ cover model while she wore unflattering pajamas and reeked of burnt plastic.

After a tedious extrication from Shelley's bear hug, he

marched forward. "Need a boost, Dulcina?"

His continued use of that god-awful name baffled her. Even her parents and sister had switched to calling her Sweets, but this guy couldn't seem to wrap his mind around the preference. Of course, the three syllables somehow gained a hint of sexiness when he said it in that Southern drawl. The word rolled off his tongue with a lilting musicality that appealed to some traitorous part of her psyche, the unwelcome effect getting on her nerves in a big way.

On top of that, the weird physical reaction she had to his mere presence irritated her. Ever since she'd hit puberty, being within five feet of the boy she'd known all her life—one who'd since grown into a gorgeous twenty-five-year-old man—did weird shit to random body parts. Her cheeks burned, her breath quickened, her palms got sweaty, and her heart rate turned erratic. The smug grin he wore, along with the patronizing tone he'd used, earned her best friend's half sibling a temporary place on Sweets' list of least-favorite uninvited guests. "You're blocking my view."

He offered his hand. "Of what?"

"Water damage." Before she could accept his assistance, the empty space between them distorted. Transparent, flickering waves created a blur, as if two realities had shifted out of sync. Frozen in place by the premonition's onslaught, she watched a version of herself meet his palm with her own. Their fingers twined, and he hoisted her up too fast. When she crashed into his chest, his arms lowered to circle her waist.

He drew her closer. She tilted her head back and parted her lips. A storm brewed in the depths of his almost-black eyes, coloring them with swirls of white and gray. A light furrow formed between his brows, certainty and possession lending his face a dangerous edge.

Alarm bells ringing in her ears, she blinked away the vision and clenched her hands into fists. Keeping them at her sides, she did a full sit-up. Talk about a close call. "Thanks for taking care of the smoke. It even smells nice in here now."

Lines bracketed the sides of his mouth. He scrutinized her through narrowed eyes, as if he somehow suspected she'd altered their course. "No problem. I haven't used magic in weeks."

Thanks to copious at-home ab exercises, she managed to curl onto her feet in a single lithe move. Pivoting to lean against the wall, she crossed her arms. She'd avoided a disaster by a split second; it seemed prudent to keep a wary distance from its source. "I don't know what Enforcement's manual says, but you can't just show up at people's homes."

He stepped forward, crowding into her personal space. "Please tell me you don't *still* think the Council is the source of all evil." It could be her guilty conscience, but a different accusation leadened the air.

"You could've called ahead." She had to concentrate to keep her voice from shaking.

Trotting over to stand next to her, Shelley patted his upper arm and dispelled the tension. "Don't be silly." With a frown of concentration, she continued in a horrible accent. *"Mi casa es su casa,"* which sounded closer to "Mee case-ahh isa sua case-ahh." While she absorbed vocabulary with robot-like efficacy, her butchering of pronunciation would make any native speaker cringe.

"¡Como el infierno!" Sweets muttered under her breath.

Shelley turned to stare at her. "What does *that* mean? I'm on Rosetta Stone Spanish Level 3, and I still haven't learned it."

The woman's brother coughed. "Pretty sure it's not in the curriculum. *En Inglés, por favor.* I took French in high school, remember?" To her relief, his tone had lost its calculating edge.

Sweets directed her answer at Shelley. "Like hell is our house his house. I won't have some Enforcement agent nosing around my things." She turned and jabbed her finger into his chest. "You want to visit, you schedule ahead." That way, she could find an excuse not to be home—starting right this instant.

A clueless giggle from Shelley's direction interrupted her mental planning. "You're being ridiculous. He's family."

Sweets looked down at the witch's covered toes. Stomping on them with her bare foot would do too little damage. "I'll believe it when you get a DNA test."

Judging from appearances, few would believe these siblings shared a mother. Mikal's skin was several shades darker than Shelley's, his six-foot-tall broad-chested build dwarfing his sister's diminutive height. Shelley had luscious curves with plenty of padding, while her brother's lean body consisted of bone and rippling muscle. His military-cut hair was a dull, coarse slate, which contrasted with Shelley's maple curls. The earth mage's round cheeks and button nose ensured she looked nothing like her brother, who had high slanting cheekbones, a prominent nasal bridge, and a square jaw. Chocolate-brown eyes and thick, pouting lips numbered among the few commonalities these purported blood relations shared.

Mikal cleared his throat. "By the way, I *did* call. Both your phones are out of credit. They went straight to voicemail. It's why Mom sent me over here after I dropped by her place."

Shelley hit her forehand with the heel of her hand. "I knew I'd forgotten something."

It didn't matter, since they couldn't afford to refill their accounts. Glancing at the shrapnel-decorated floor, Sweets rounded up the hundred-or-so pieces of metal with a wave of her hand and sent them into the trash can. With Mikal around, her telekinesis got supercharged. "As you can see, we're doing fine. Can you go away now?"

He stepped closer and chucked his knuckles under her chin. "Why so grumps, kitty cat? Haven't had your morning coffee?"

Come to think of it, lack of caffeine might have a great deal to do with her sour mood. "No. And I guess I'm not having any for a while." The thought of surviving the mornings without her usual boost almost gave her a panic attack.

He glanced at his sister. "I saw the stack of stuff by the door, which, by the way, you guys didn't lock...."

Seeing her friend's eyes narrow, Sweets grinned. Because he'd lived in New York for the past four years, Shelley at times forgot how annoying and overbearing the man could be. Distance had made his sister's heart grow fonder, but it wouldn't take long before his meddlesome ways wore on her nerves. When they did, the witch would evict him from the house without needing a single prompt. "We don't even share a dad, so you'd better not start acting like one again," Shelley warned.

The muscle on his jaw ticked. The siblings had fought like cats and dogs growing up. Before a series of unfortunate premonitions had prompted Sweets to limit their in-person interactions, she'd played the peacemaker between him and her best friend, which she still did quite often on the phone and over e-mail.

To her surprise, Shelley's overprotective arch nemesis lifted his hands in a gesture of surrender. "It's a neutral observation, little sis. Lock the door, don't lock the door. Hell, leave it open so snow and ice can blow in—it's your house."

On the verge of giving him a high five of respect, Sweets winced when he continued, "About the bills—I can give you two a few bucks to get you through the year."

"We don't need your money." A chunk of the ceiling fell and hit the counter, dimming the effect of Shelley's feigned confidence by a significant margin. Nonetheless, the witch squared her shoulders. "We've got everything under control."

Sweets turned to glare at her business partner for the non-royal use of the word *we*. No one should stand between her and a working phone and morning coffee. Turning her hand palm up, she cleared her throat. "If she won't take it, I will." She'd deal with the consequences of owing him a favor later. She'd be stupid to turn down an opportunity to get them enough liquidity to survive the week. Besides, he'd be giving her a loan, not a handout.

Shelley bumped Sweets' shoulder. "Stay out of this."

"You stay out of it. This is between me and the Enforcement loan shark."

The witch's sharp elbow dug into her stomach. "You don't even *like* him. Why are you taking his side?"

Sweets batted her eyelashes. "Survival."

"What happened to being independent and self-sufficient?" Shelley forced out a fake smile. "We're in this together. It's been our joint New Year's resolution for four years. It's bad enough you got Cat to do our taxes for free."

How could the witch still not be over that after eight whole months? Sweets had indulged almost all of her friend's pigheaded warped ethics, but she'd drawn the line at paying for TurboTax when her sister was a certified public accountant.

Before the argument could go down a well-traveled tangent, Shelley's much saner sibling had the decency to step in. "Come on, ladies. Don't fight. As the one dude here, it makes me uncomfortable. What if I charge interest?"

Her lower lip sticking out, Shelley shook her head. "Thank you, but no. I'm a grownup. You should start treating me like one."

Easy for her to say. The woman lived off the fruits and vegetables she grew, brewed tea comprised of dried mint leaves, and hadn't left the house in a year. Though they didn't need to pay rent, the soon-to-be condemned cottage Shelley had inherited from her grandmother happened to be smack dab in a preppy neighborhood in Northern Virginia, with property taxes so high they ate up the lion's share of last year's profits. While Sweets also drank the financial-independence Kool-Aid, having a working microwave topped her list of priorities. No way would she let pride get in the way of Lean Cuisine.

She beamed a smile at one of the three people in the world from whom she didn't mind requesting aid. "Can you spare a hundred bucks? I'll pay you back in a week. We sold a ton of stuff over Christmas, but PayPal's got server issues, and the money's stuck. We'd have been fine if the microwave hadn't blown, but— Ouch!"

Sweets rubbed her lower back, where a bruise was likely forming. "Seriously, *chica*, stop acting like a baby."

The woman's brother also seemed to have had enough. He took possession of Sweets' upper arm and propelled them out of the kitchen, across the tiny living room, and through the front door in five wind-assisted leaps. Hot on their heels, Shelley skidded to a stop at the entryway, where he shut the thick wood barrier in her face.

"Whoa, that's plain mean." Slipping her feet into the snow boots she'd discarded by the door, Sweets rubbed her bare arms to stave off the biting cold. "You know she can't leave the house." Shelley's power had gotten stronger with age, but the magical equivalent of agoraphobia had accompanied the increase. It'd gotten bad enough during the past year she couldn't go out and about.

He shrugged. "You've always been the less-crazy one. I need to hit the ATM. Why don't you warm up in the car and let me buy you a cup of coffee?"

With that offer dangling in front of her face, what self-respecting caffeine-addicted witch could say no?

Chapter Two

Sweets shook her head as she waited inside Mikal's Chevy Tahoe. The guy couldn't be more obvious about working for Enforcement. She didn't know why Council folk loved these clunky SUVs. It might be reliable and useful on an IKEA trip, but a car should say something about its owner. Given, the man who'd driven her to Starbucks could be counted on for unfailing support and would come in handy if she ever got around to buying furniture, but he was by no means generic. He deserved to drive something memorable—something unique—and not a soulless means of getting from point A to point B.

If she ever scraped together enough cash to buy a car, it'd be a Beetle or a Mini Cooper, and she'd never pair black-leather seats with the same color exterior. Being stuck in this monochromatic pristine box threatened to give her hives.

When had he become the epitome of boring? She missed the boy who'd annoyed all their neighbors with his motorcycle, the guy who got her and Shelley their first fake IDs. Ever since he'd morphed into a responsible peon, had a security clearance, and drew a steady paycheck, his mere existence turned her into an unsuccessful loser by comparison.

Playing with the seatbelt's metal clasp, she looked up through the sunroof. Light glinted into her eyes, and, in a hazy precognitive rush, the glass was gone.

The sky shifted from bright blue to an ebony expanse dotted with white twinkling stars. The car's confines should have been cold, but a warm circling breeze licked her skin. She sat on the same seat, facing the opposite direction. Bare shoulders occupied her vision; strong hard legs rippled under her ass. Cinnamon, mint, and sweat filled her lungs, all laced with an undertone of pine. She kissed a beard-covered jaw, trailed her lips down a corded neck, and explored a muscled chest the color of chocolate.

Calloused palms slid up her back. Strong sure fingers unhooked her bra and smoothed the straps off her shoulders. Coarse facial hair rasped over her nipple before a hot, wet mouth closed over it and sucked. Her shoulder blades hit the dashboard. His swirling tongue feasted on her breast. His hand shoved her legs apart.

He circled her clit with his thumb, pulsing over it until her head rolled back. She spotted fireworks through the glass, flashes of red, white, and blue reflecting off rippling water. Her own voice echoed in her ears—pleas she'd never dreamed of voicing.

Two thick fingers filled her, spreading as she spasmed. A scream ripped from her throat. "Mi—"

The door opened with the quiet click characteristic of new cars, shattering her erotic daydream. Her breaths shallow and her panties damp, she dug her nails into the leather beneath her hands. The back of her head met the seat. She'd never experienced a vision that vivid—one lush with scent, sight, touch, and sound.

With a frowning glance, the vehicle's owner slid inside and handed her a cardboard cup. "This should get you in a better mood."

Wiping sweat off her forehead despite the nippy air, she accepted the huge container. Nothing would come of the premonition—as nothing had come of all the ones that came before. She'd broken her rule and allowed them to be alone in an enclosed space. She wouldn't make the same mistake again any time soon.

Taking a calming breath, she focused on sounding as normal as possible. "How's this a regular coffee?"

"I got you what you always get in winter—a venti pumpkin-spice latte." He sealed them in and started the engine. With the turn of a knob, heated air hit the tree-shaped freshener. Its scent mingled with his spicy aftershave. After that vision, she almost moaned at the imagery the smell invoked. She'd been sexually frustrated to begin with, and having him so close propelled her libido into overdrive.

Fanning her burning face, she grumbled, "It's not what I asked for."

"Don't be such a cheapskate. I told you, it's my treat." He settled against the backrest, his head angled in her direction. Sipping his drink, he released a long breath, the corners of his lips lifting to form an expression of pure bliss.

Her nipples tightened into sharp peaks, and she doubted the cold had caused it. "Thanks, but—"

"My sister's brainwashed you, hasn't she? How about you buy me a triple-shot espresso in a few weeks?"

She tried to wrangle her thoughts back into some semblance of coherence. "Nice try. You'll be back in New York in a day or two." If not, she'd self-admit into an insane asylum.

"Sure about that?" He looked too smug for comfort.

An unprecedented flood of excitement and elation threw her off balance. What the hell? She should be scared shitless, not so happy she almost jumped out of her seat at the thought of him quitting. "Enforcement doesn't operate in the District—not in the open, anyway."

"Things change."

Pure unadulterated fear eliminated any lingering embers of desire. "Since when?"

His brows drew together. "Since a fire mage short-circuited a hotel elevator and ice sculptures of Godzilla made headlines. Why are you freaking out?"

She had two reasons but chose to voice the less-important

one. "Why do you think? If they find out—"

"There's no *they*. It's just me." He tapped her cup's plastic cover. "Drink this before it gets cold."

Her brain ceasing to function at optimum levels, she savored the bittersweet drink of the gods. She needed an exit plan, pronto. None came to mind. "So, you'll cover for me?"

He shook his head. "Nope. You'll register. You're not a scared fourteen-year-old anymore. You want to be an adult? Instead of insisting I can't pay for your coffee, own up to what you are."

Beads of cold sweat chilled her forehead. "They'll take me away—lock me up in some white building—"

"Not on my watch. I've worked for them long enough to know they won't force you into anything you don't want. You'll have to get tested at the Institute, they'll ask me to keep an eye on you, but they're not monsters, they're—"

"Old-school, black-caped, cauldron-stirring, out-of-touch-with-reality warlocks and witches who still believe in blood pentagrams and animal sacrifice." Her hand shook hard enough she had to lower the coffee to her lap.

He raised his gaze to the clear tempered-glass roof. "Where do you witches get these conspiracy theories? Do I look like I own a cauldron?"

The image of him cackling over a bubbling potion managed to calm her nerves. Another influx of hot liquid steadied her enough to stem the shakes. He'd never hurt her, not even for the Council. As for the other problem, she'd figure something out. "It's all over the Internet."

"Which you know is the most reliable source of information."

She didn't appreciate his sarcasm. "I've read blogs...."

"And I've researched this—from the inside—for years. I'm certain nothing bad will happen to you. Besides, you're a damned foreseer. You'd know ahead of time if there's danger."

She hated it when he relied on logic and facts to win arguments. "As you can tell from my dead microwave, premonitions don't give me much of a head start."

"But you trust my judgment." His complete self-assurance tempted her to splash the damn coffee in his face. "I know what I'm talking about, so for the love of all that's holy, register, relax, and get on with your life. The Council isn't perfect, Enforcement's fucking inefficient, but they're here to protect the magical community. No one is out to get you, and they won't lock you up or make you use your powers for evil. Did I cover all the accusations flying around the electronic rumor mill?"

Since she couldn't come up with a clever retort, she chugged her beverage. While irrational fear continued to turn her stomach, the sensible side of her gave his argument significant weight. When she'd first run to him in tears after a vision of blood and death, they'd looked up a bunch of stuff online and agreed to stay quiet. Years later, he seemed convinced they had nothing to worry about—something she'd suspected for a while. "I'll think about it."

She almost dropped her cup when he shrugged and stopped pushing. "That's all I'm asking."

She stared at him. "Okay, the *real* Midnight would never back off like that. Who are you, and what've you done to him?"

He chuckled. "We keep on missing each other, so we've met—what—a couple dozen times over the past three years? You spent most of it nagging me to quit my job, so of course we argued. If you haven't noticed, neither of us is a teenager anymore. This is your life. Take as much time as you need to think things through."

She wrinkled her nose. "God, you sound so...sensible. It's great you're moving here, but I don't think we'll get along. I'm an irresponsible loser. Sitting in this car with you is destroying my cred."

He pinched her cheek. "Says Little Ms. Small Business Owner who doesn't splurge on Starbucks. While we're on the subject, why won't you let me spot you more than a hundred dollars so you can, I don't know, afford a deadbolt?"

As if keeping the five twenty-dollar bills he'd handed her earlier wasn't bad enough. "I'm a witch who can see the future.

Shells sets off explosions without even trying. I'd love to see a burglar break in."

"And if I gift you and Shelley a Nespresso machine as a belated Christmas present...."

"The pods cost almost a buck each. Do I look like I'm swimming in cash?" Noticing his peeved expression, she gave an inch. "If you're looking for ways to spend your Christmas bonus, I've been eyeing this blowtorch...."

He groaned. "Live a little, will you? All you two ever ask for are gardening and jewelry supplies. It's gotten so out of hand, I had to listen to Mom complain for half an hour this morning."

She'd never understood why Shelley and her entire family preferred waking up at half-past four. It didn't make a lick of sense, and by the time Sweets got out of bed, they'd already have had three hours' worth of arguments. "So the guy who tutored me through calculus is telling me to be less responsible?"

With a melodramatic sigh, he polished off the last of his drink and held his hand out for her empty cup. Lowering the window with the push of a button, he aimed the cardboard cylinders at a trash can a few feet away. After he tossed them both in the air, they landed in the metal mesh confines with the aid of a few gusts of wind.

Closing the window, he pulled his seat belt across his chest. "I need to be somewhere at nine, but I'll be back. Got any plans tonight? I can come over, cook dinner, and weasel my way into Shelley's good graces with some chocolate cake."

She'd have said yes if he'd pitched this to her ten minutes ago. After that little pheromone-filled trip, she wouldn't let him near her any time after sunset. "You might want to give Shells a few more days to cool down, and New Year's Eve is the best time to hawk jewelry." When he opened his mouth, she lifted a finger. "I would invite you over later, but I sort of have a date."

On Halloween, she'd gifted her sister a one-night stand from an online dating company run by the mysterious Madame Eve. Before Cat left on her romantic getaway, she'd given the same service to Sweets as a joke. A vellum invitation for tonight had showed up in this morning's mail, indicating she should meet her date at a New Year's Eve party at the Castillo Waterfront Hotel.

Since the hookup came with all-you-can-drink champagne and happened to be located in the capital's busiest shopping district, she didn't see the harm in showing up. If the guy turned out lame, she'd bail after indulging in some free bubbly. Either way, she'd get a much-needed distraction from the weird, fucked-up situation between her and Mikal.

"I didn't know you had a boyfriend. What's he like?"

Even the threat of a ruined friendship couldn't make her tell him an outright lie. "No idea. I've never met him before. Someone else set it up."

Something about the way his forehead wrinkled suggested he didn't approve. "Don't forget to load up your phone. Give me a call if he gets frisky."

She burst out laughing. Thank God he still treated her like a naughty little sister. "Dude—if the guy so much as looks at me the wrong way, I'll put him on the floor myself. I've buffed up since you left, and this whole foresight business gives me a half-second advantage. I don't want to brag, but I've been kicking ass and taking names. Go find some poor defenseless victim to hover over."

◌੪

Mikal resisted the urge to flinch when Jackson Frost the Second looked up from the Enforcement transfer papers. The sixty-five-year-old Director of the Clandestine Affairs Agency reeked of old magic. Operating under the cover of a flourishing legal practice, the Mage's Council's spymaster oversaw all supernatural matters in Washington, D.C. The CAA kept an eye on human governments, and its director played an obscure advisory role on the magical community's governing body.

The floor-to-ceiling windows of Frost's corner office showed off an icy K Street lined with piles of muddy snow. The city's financial, legal, and corporate center, the area consisted of steel-and-glass skyscrapers, gridlocked streets, and expensive cars. Along the dark Metro stairs and in shadowed shop corners, the homeless begged for scraps as lobbyists in expensive suits buzzed by without pause.

With witches and warlocks forming an unreported extreme minority in America, the Council had to limit its footprint in the hub of human power. Until recently, the arrangement came with no downsides. For the past century, the District's sterile and almost soulless atmosphere had deterred migration from blue-blooded magical families who preferred more vibrant cities like New Orleans, New York, Charleston, Atlanta, Los Angeles, and San Francisco. The majority of mages who lived around the capital either had roots going back to the Mayflower or had immigrated from foreign countries where persecution was an issue. Both types went out of their way to maintain an inconspicuous lifestyle.

But the recent economic downturn had drawn college graduates from all corners of the nation to D.C., one of the few regions with rising demand for educated labor. With the Spanish Inquisition and Salem Witch Trials footnotes in textbooks, the country's magical youth continued to test the boundaries of their parents' traditional shadows. The Clandestine Affairs Agency didn't have enough bandwidth to police the city, and the complete absence of an official law and order representative here had spelled trouble.

Clearing his throat, Mikal broke the uncomfortable silence. "I hope everything is in order, sir."

"You have the necessary qualifications." Frost didn't sound too pleased. Perhaps to make a transfer as difficult as possible, the warlock refused to allow any Council employee to operate in his city outside the umbrella of his law firm, which housed the analytical and administrative branches of the CAA. To fit into this surface-level cover, an agent must possess a law degree and pass an exam to become a patent attorney. Due to bureaucratic politics, Enforcement refused to fund the pursuit of either, so the city had been left without its presence.

To come here, Mikal had obtained the necessary credentials on his own time and at his own expense. Under Frost, he'd be expected to work full-time as a lawyer on top of fulfilling his role as the magical community's sheriff. Thank God the supernatural population here remained relatively low. "If you have everything you need, I'll be back next week...."

"Don't be ridiculous, boy. You'll start today." Pressing the intercom button, Frost barked, "Send Ms. Mao here in fifteen minutes with new-hire paperwork." Without waiting for any indication there'd been someone on the other end of the line, he hung up. "Tell me, why did you join Enforcement? According to these files, you're a dissident."

Of course, the damned spook would run a thorough background check. "That's an exaggeration. I once wrote a few articles in an underground college newspaper. Didn't we all do stupid things as kids?"

The warlock drummed his fingers on a manila folder marked *CLASSIFIED—FYEO—NO FORN*. Why the CAA would deem Mikal's personnel record a matter of Council security, he didn't know.

"You took the Enforcement test when you turned twenty-one. A curious choice, for someone with your virulent opinions."

Mikal had answered this question several-hundred times while strapped to an empath on one hand and a telepath on the other. Nonetheless, the issue came up at every stage of his career. "The best way to find out if the rumors about the Council are true is to become part of it. For personal reasons, I'd been curious."

Frost narrowed those creepy mercury eyes. "You have someone you want to protect."

"Don't we all? After four years in Enforcement, I've confirmed the conspiracy theories pertinent to my situation to be a load of b...lies. The rest doesn't keep me up at night."

"And why did you want to come to D.C.?"

He'd been prepared for this question. Spies had a reputation for paranoia, and Mikal had worked days and studied nights for four long years to obtain what most would consider a lateral move. "I have family in the area. It's home."

One corner of the warlock's mouth curved up. But for a few light lines, the man had a smooth, chiseled visage and the complexion of a marble sculpture. "I have a boy your age. He works here, and I haven't seen him in weeks."

Since spending five minutes in this office threatened to give Mikal frostbite, he couldn't blame the man. To avoid insult, he equivocated. "I get along with my younger sister."

"But you must prefer New York to here."

Mikal shifted in the leather chair designed for discomfort. Two inches closer to the floor than normal, the non-adjustable seat squeaked at his slightest movement.

Compared to the District's monotony, the Big Apple was the shiny center of magic, culture, entertainment, and art. But no matter how much fun he had there, none of the experiences seemed complete. Each almost-perfect moment lacked any fulfillment, as if a crucial piece of the kaleidoscopic puzzle had gone missing.

Though the holidays he'd spent at home had been a boring flurry of home-cooked meals, jogs through the park, and trips to the grocery store, he preferred them to the pale facsimile of contentment he'd achieved in New York. He'd smiled more this morning than he had in months. "On the contrary. I wouldn't want to live anywhere else. And from a career standpoint, this is a place where I can make a name. A good number of young witches and warlocks have flocked here, not all of them the kind who'll stay under the radar. Someone needs to be around to remind them about the consequences—to prevent minor magical accidents from turning into catastrophes."

Frost lifted a snow-white eyebrow. "None of those things have happened on my watch."

"Yet." When his future boss squinted, Mikal cleared his throat. "Having to police the city is a drain on Clandestine Affairs' resources. Your operatives are trained to dig up secrets, not keep a bunch of teenage as—idiots out of trouble."

Frost snorted. "Do I look like I have men to spare? Someone's been keeping kids from blowing things up, but it's not us."

The revelation came as a surprise. Enforcement assumed Frost had been spreading his assets around. For the past couple of years, the low level of serious supernatural crime had been statistically anomalous. "Did you investigate?"

The warlock placed his elbows on the giant mahogany desk and formed a triangle with his hands. "If some masked bimbo wants to play vigilante for free, I'm not going to stop her. That's your job. But if you run into the witch, send her my way. I hate female operatives—they end up popping out babies and wasting my time—but having someone around with breasts has its uses."

With that sales pitch, Mikal doubted any woman would sign on. He'd noticed the conspicuous lack of female lawyers in the firm, and, according to Council records, the male-to-female ratio among operatives in the CAA hovered around eight to one. Even Enforcement had made more progress with their employment practices.

"Do you have any more information on this vigilante besides the person's gender? It would be useful. We're bound to run into each other." To be specific, Mikal planned on hunting the chick down and threatening her with an obstruction-of-justice charge. He considered few things more dangerous than untrained civilians running around, pretending to be superheroes. Best-case scenario, they got in the way. Worst-case scenario, they got themselves killed.

Frost shrugged. "Not much. Late teens or early twenties. Between five-four and five-seven. Non-elemental. Skinny. Brunette. Brown eyes. Hispanic. Mouths off and wears a black-leather eye mask."

"Huh." Ill at ease for a reason he couldn't quite tease apart, Mikal stored away the information. The description fit several hundred people in the D.C.-Metro area. "I'll keep an eye out. Anything else I should know before I start?"

The spymaster drummed his fingers against each other. "You've been instructed to carbon copy me on all incident reports and loop me into all ongoing investigations?"

Working for the Council amounted to 70 percent paperwork, 25 percent meetings, and 5 percent actual work. "Of course."

The answer seemed to satisfy. Frost pulled out a drawer, rummaged, and tossed a red envelope onto the desk's glass surface. "Since I'm stuck with you, here's your first assignment. Show up there tonight and report back."

An Enforcement agent on loan to Clandestine Affairs shouldn't have to take on additional duties, but an evening's work seemed a fair price for an olive branch. Besides, the day-job salary he'd be pocketing from Frost and Sons was twice his current pay.

Pulling out a thick piece of vellum from the crimson sleeve, he read the text out loud as confirmation. "Madame Eve cordially invites you to a one-night stand. Your mystery date will meet you at the Castillo Waterfront Hotel's New Year's Eve Party at 10:00 p.m." Furrowing his brows, he inquired, "You want me to investigate a prostitution ring? This seems like a job for the local cops, unless these are magical escorts. Even then, as long as they're discreet...."

Frost scowled. "Who gives a shit about hookers? This is a fact-finding mission. Two employees here, both warlocks, fell victim to this purported dating service. I signed you up before you transferred to see what would happen. If your one true love shows up tonight, then we're dealing with a run-of-the-mill matchmaker. Nothing I can do about that. If someone attempts to use mind control, you're trained to detect and resist. Either way, I want to know why some French witch is targeting me."

"By fell victim, you mean...."

"The works." The warlock's fist landed on his desk. "Lowered efficiency, more time on the phone, vacation requests, you name it. They're dropping like flies, and my bottom line is suffering."

Mikal wouldn't categorize two employees finding romance as dropping like flies, but he'd gain nothing from contradicting the man signing one of his paychecks. "So, she's been going after clandestine operatives?"

"No, they're both dimwits with more magic than sense. I wouldn't recruit them to work for the CAA in a million years."

"Okay, then why—?"

The warlock's hand met tempered glass. "Spies don't make me money. They eke out their minimum billings and flit away to stalk fancy dinner parties. Both these victims were attorneys in their prime." White frost spread from the point of impact to cover the entire surface. "I had a decade of eighty-hour work weeks left in them, but lately they've both cut back. My own son's threatening to quit unless I dial him down to sixty hours. Pah. At the boy's age, I worked twice that. All this because he wants to spend more time with his new piece on the side—some bimbo he hasn't even bothered to introduce to his father."

Mikal straightened his tie. If he'd been in this kid's shoes, he would turn in his resignation and move to Bermuda. Frost had better not expect the same lack of work-life balance from him. "I see."

The warlock's liquid-silver eyes glinted. "No, you don't see. Look, boy, this Council business is well and good, but my first priority isn't them, it's my bank account. God knows there's nothing I can change if they're fated pairs, but if it's some sort of brain-addling spell, then I want to bloody undo it—starting with my son."

When a soft knock interrupted their chitchat, Mikal heaved a sigh of relief. He didn't care why Frost tasked him to do this. Wild goose chase or not, he planned on filing for overtime.

Chapter Three

*D*ulcina's grumpy voice crackled over the speaker. "Leo? I thought you guys were on vacation? Did Cat not like the ring?"

Mikal settled into the creaky rolling office chair. Unlike his boss's suite, this closet-sized room had no windows, came with a circa 1940s desk, and the computer still ran Windows XP. For reasons he didn't quite understand, a tape recorder hooked up to a microphone sat next to his keyboard. "Umm...it's me. Who's this Leo person?"

"That's weird. I swear the Caller ID said Frost and Sons. My phone must be glitching." She sounded guilty, confirming his suspicion she'd rejected the calls he'd placed on his mobile. Despite her outward surliness, she'd almost bounced with glee when he told her about moving back. Her smile erased several years' worth of lethargy. She might not know it yet, but he'd come home for her.

With the demographic tide shifting faster than the Council's antiquated views, Enforcement's presence in the nation's capital would soon grow to match the influx. He intended to establish seniority by then, putting him in a position to take command. Though he hadn't lied to her earlier, he'd omitted one key finding. The Council kept tabs on precogs because of their predilection to get into trouble, and the Registry's intent might be to protect. But both Enforcement and the CAA wouldn't shy away from embroiling a foreseer in dangerous situations. Coming out of the closet would bring her no harm as long as he had the power to dictate the terms of her involvement. His elemental command hadn't been mature enough to make the old guard hesitate three years ago.

It was now.

"This *is* Frost and Sons. Are you dating someone here, too?" The thought of her going out with a sleaze-bag lawyer prompted him to scowl at the dusty LCD screen. Though he planned on taking his time getting her to come around, he had no intention of letting another guy swoop in.

They weren't just friends—never had been and never would be—and they'd danced around this simple, scary truth for far too long. He didn't know when things had changed, but sometime over the past dozen years, he stopped seeing her as a second little sister.

In their teens, her crush on him had been damn annoying. Many a youthful necking session in his parents' garage had come to an abrupt end when he'd glimpsed a scrawny brown kitten skulking amidst the shelved containers. By his junior year in high school, he'd developed the habit of searching his bedroom before a date showed up, lest he risked a feline voyeur.

To his relief, she'd matured enough to back off the summer before his senior year. Then he'd left for college, and, with each return visit, the four-year age gap that had seemed like a giant canyon to a seventeen-year-old boy, narrowed to an insignificant pothole.

His intense attraction to her had smacked him in the head three years before on this very day. The dynamic duo had joined him in the Big Apple to witness the famed New Year's Eve celebration at Times Square. Having joked about needing someone to lock lips with at the end of the countdown, he and Sweets had made a pact to save each other from loser-dom. When people started yelling numbers, she'd stared up at him with an unmistakable invitation etched on her expressive face. He'd bent his head as she leaned in, the scent of his own shampoo wafting off her sable hair. If an accident hadn't sent the drink in her hand crashing into his chest, he didn't know what would have happened when the fireworks went off.

Stunned by his reaction to a girl less than two months over eighteen, he'd taken great care to keep his distance. But the lost moment forced him to sift through memories of their past, when she'd worn braces and walked around with paint smudges on her face. The nature of their bond shifted with such subtlety neither of them noticed, but, in hindsight, the truth was impossible to miss. Even in their youth, his feelings toward her hadn't been platonic.

And now she'd grown into a veritable head turner. Though she didn't have an hourglass silhouette by any stretch of the imagination, he'd glimpsed subtle curves under her tank top and shorts. He'd gone hard at the sight the small dark circles topping her pert breasts, just barely pulled back his hand from touching her gorgeous golden skin. Silky smooth and glowing with health, the swells above her neckline invited a man to taste and mark, and he loathed the idea of any other guy getting his paws on her.

His erection had strained the confines of his briefs the moment he showed up at her place and found her on the kitchen floor, her chest heaving and her shoulder-length hair spread in a dark halo behind her. Those doe eyes, framed by thick fringes of sooty lashes, had transfixed him for at least half a minute. Then he'd gotten distracted by the rest of her.

He'd been thankful she'd refused his offer to help her up. If she'd touched him, he'd no idea what he might have done in that state. As he watched her curl onto tiny bare feet, his intention had firmed into hard resolve. His training had taught him the value of patience. He'd spend the next few months lulling her into a false sense of safety. Once she lowered her guard, he'd make his move.

"Since when are you so obsessed with my love life? Leo's my sister's boyfriend, asshat. He calls me to find out what to bribe her with. Why are you at his law firm?" Thank God, talking to her on the phone took their explosive chemistry out of the equation. With her elfin face away from view, she remained the girl he'd grown up with—one of the few females on the planet he counted as a close friend. Instead of coming up with stupid excuses and scampering away, she'd talk to him at length with laughter tingeing her voice.

"It's my day job. You know how it works. The higher-ups can't afford to pay anyone full-time." Since this wasn't a secure line, he left it at that. He'd tell her the details in person.

She took the hint and switched subjects. "How's your first day at work? Is it as shitty as I think it is?"

Glancing at the austere white walls and piles of file folders on the worn carpet, he groaned. "Worse. It's an effing plantation over here."

"That's what you said about your...umm...night job."

He'd thought Enforcement was bad, but Clandestine Affairs made the overt side seem like the poster agency for equal employment opportunities. "I'm the token black lawyer—and by that I mean the only one. In the attorney pool, there's me, thirty some white guys, and one woman. Wanna know the support staff breakdown?"

"I already do. I'm pals with your HR person. They're all chicks except for the mailroom people—brunettes with a sprinkling of blondes."

Disappointed, he sank into the backrest. He'd been looking forward to offloading his complaints. Even while they'd lived in different cities, they called each other at least once a week to catch up. He chatted with her more over the phone than any member of his actual family. "How did you and Ms. Mao even meet?" While in the same age bracket, the petite Asian witch seemed too serious to run in Sweets' artsy circle.

"Call her Mina already—Ms. Mao sounds like some Chinese dictator's daughter. We took the same night classes a while back. By the way, I need you to confirm her story. Do they *really* use dictation machines there?"

He glanced at the microphone on his desk. Mystery solved. "Yup. In full tape-recorder glory." His focus shifted to the beginning of her statement. "You didn't tell me you're getting a master's." Though smart enough to complete a B.A. in three years while working full-time, she hated structured learning.

"I'm not. Remember the business and accounting lessons I bitched about—the ones I took to keep *Mamà* happy? She's still convinced Cat and I will both have PhDs one day. Talk about delusional."

Was it any wonder their mothers got along? "No sympathy here. I'm the one with two parents who both think I'm taking the scenic route to med school."

She laughed. Their families' lack of understanding when it came to unorthodox career paths had always given them something in common. Out of love and respect, they'd both gone to great lengths to live up to unrealistic expectations. Remembering how difficult it had been to step off the pre-paved path, he admired the courage it took for her to chase dreams of her own.

"I forgot to ask. Where's your blind date?" He wanted to keep tabs on her tonight, but activating the GPS tracker on her phone seemed like overkill.

"Georgetown, which is where I've pitched my stall. I have to say—I'm making bank. I might even pay you back tomorrow *and* buy you those espresso shots. When the partygoers start funneling into clubs, I'll pack up and head over to meet the potential love of my life."

For once, the stars aligned to his convenience. "I'll be at the waterfront working until around eleven." He couldn't envision this fake date lasting any longer than an hour. Once he verified the setup involved no mind control, he'd bail. "If the guy's a loser, you can ditch him and come watch the fireworks with me."

Her forced laugh held a hint of nervousness. "I plan on getting tipsy long before midnight, boy-o. I'll pass on the chaperone. Besides, this is a hookup. My standards are pretty low these days. This city's the worst place to be single—they've done statistical studies to prove it and stuff."

He opened his mouth to start a lecture before biting his

tongue. She'd dig in her heels if he sounded even remotely bossy. "How do you plan on getting back? I can't drink on duty, so I might as well give you a ride home and save you the cab fare. Tell me where you'll be."

"So you can stalk me, scare off my date, and stop me from having my first real drink in months?" she challenged, her voice a tad too high-pitched. "No thank you."

He scratched his head. She'd seen him in action a few too many times. "All I'm offering is to be your designated driver. Have as many wine coolers as you want."

"I'm twenty-one, not fifteen. I'm drinking champagne, and lots of it." Her words tumbled out almost too fast for coherence. "Having your ugly mug staring at me from around the corner crimps my style. I remember what you did to any schmuck who came within ten feet of Shelley."

In his defense, none of those idiots had been good enough to sniff around his baby sister. "Why are you so gung ho about dating all of a sudden?" While Shelley had enjoyed wrapping unsuspecting males around her little finger growing up, Dulcina had always shied away from boys. She'd joined him for a *Farscape* marathon on her prom night after laughing off his offer to escort her to the dance, which she'd termed an overpriced excuse to bump uglies.

"I want to make sure everything's working down there."

Talk about too much information. "For my sanity, can you text me at eleven so I know everything's on the up and up?"

"Sheesh, fine. You have an actual sibling to get all weird around, you know?"

"She can't find trouble if she won't leave the house." Shelley's condition came with a single perk. Sighing, he tried to slow his accelerated heart rate. The desk's scratched wooden surface didn't look like it could withstand a hard punch or tornado-force winds. "I'll call you as soon as I'm off the clock. Don't do anything stupid." Or sleep with the guy, unless she wanted the unfortunate fool to end up dangling from the top of the Washington Monument.

"My phone's on and charged, and I'll run home if the man even talks funny, all right? Gotta go. I spot Japanese tourists with fancy cameras and money to burn."

Staring at the old phone long after it disconnected, he pulled out his Enforcement cell and dialed headquarters. After all, she belonged to the magical community he'd been sent here to protect. What was the harm in gaining access to her cell's GPS on the off chance she'd need his help?

CB

Walking out of the 24-hour ATM booth onto the busy street, Sweets wrestled with the urge to lift her arms, shake her booty, and do an impromptu performance of "Who's Your Daddy?" After observing the crazy club-hopping crowd around her, she took a moment to indulge the impulse. For good measure, she topped off the short dance by leaping into the air and yelling, "Woot!"

It wasn't even midnight yet, and this had turned out to be the best New Year's Eve ever. The cash she'd deposited more than covered Flowers Forever's expenses for the next two months, and that didn't include the credit card transactions. All the coeds pre-gaming midnight frat parties had been in the mood to add some last minute oomph to their outfits, and what better complimented fireworks than jewelry? Having dispensed with most of her stock, she didn't even need to lug around cardboard boxes. The leftovers had all fit in her backpack.

Checking her watch, she marched down Wisconsin toward M Street and crossed her fingers Madame Eve's mystery one-night stand wasn't the punctual type. Already a quarter past ten, it would take her at least ten more minutes to get to the Castillo Waterfront, which meant she was on track to being half an hour late.

When her feet protested the brisk pace, she shrugged and slowed down. Rather than risk twisting her ankle in the thigh-high stiletto boots, she'd rather never meet the guy. It would be his loss, and alcohol at this point would put her to sleep anyway. She could always go home, tell Shelley the good news, and watch the fireworks on TV with some spiked coffee.

As she reached the crosswalk, red lights from a parked Metro police car glinted off a side mirror and flashed over her face. Losing her balance, she stopped and leaned against a shop window. Lowering her lids, she let the premonition wash over her.

Unlike the time she'd been in Mikal's car, she observed the event from a distance. A skinny teenage girl with ebony hair and light-brown skin struggled as a group of boys dragged her toward a dark alley. One guy had a hand over her mouth. The other four formed a human wall around them. Despite the throngs of people on the street, no one registered the attack.

They pushed her across ice-slicked pavement before shoving her onto snow-covered dirt. The following exchanges took place in a muted fast forward. Then a white flash filled her vision, followed by several strokes of lightning. When the dust cleared, five charred bodies formed a semi-circle around a screaming girl.

When the burst of foresight released her, Sweets looked up at the sky and pointed her middle finger in the air. "One night off, that's all I'm asking. It's New Year's fucking Eve."

Pulling an elastic band out of her coat pocket, she tied her hair into a high ponytail. No wonder she had a nonexistent sex life. It wasn't like she could take a personal day off from precognition, and once she foresaw something bad happening, she didn't have the heart to walk away. Add these incidents to her busy schedule and tendency to compare every man to Mikal, and she had the recipe for a twenty-one-year-old virgin.

Turning on her heel, she strode toward the high-end electronics store she'd glimpsed when her premonition began, having recognized it from her countless visits to Georgetown. About to turn into the adjacent alley, she hesitated. Since the city housed several universities, New Year's Eve brought law enforcement out in full force. With patrol cars parked at the corner of every second block, how was she supposed to handle a bunch of jocks without drawing attention? The police weren't equipped to tackle an elemental mage's electrified meltdown. Involving them risked more lives and could expose the magical community. If even a hint of this incident hit the news, the teen witch she was trying to save would land in a shitload of trouble.

While she could kick ass with the best of them, she'd come close to getting caught often enough to realize her limits. She could handle two, may be even three bad guys without too much of a ruckus. Five pushed the limits of the ten Krav Maga classes she'd taken three years ago.

Then she remembered Mikal's recent transfer. As much as she wanted to avoid him tonight, circumstances limited her options. Pulling out her phone, she called the one person she could always count on to bail her out of a jam.

"How's the date going? Need me to rescue you yet?" He sounded so eager, she almost hung up.

"Haven't got there. Look, I'm heading toward the Apple Store in G-town, the one off Wisconsin. Shit is about to happen, I'm going to stop it, and I need you to make sure the cops don't show."

"Whoa there. Stop and rewind. You're doing *what*?"

Did she have to explain everything? "Five stupid assholes are going to attack an elemental kid who can't control her powers. If I don't stop it, she'll fry them. If I stop it, the capital police will show up, and the dickwads will blab about me knocking them around with no hands. Pull some Enforcement strings to keep this off the radar until I can grab the girl and haul ass."

"Like hell." She moved the phone away from her ear before lowering the volume. Technology had its perks. "You're going to sit your skinny butt down where you are and wait fifteen minutes for me to take care of this."

She'd learned a decade before the best way to deal with the man's overprotectiveness was to ignore it. "This girl doesn't have fifteen minutes. Stay where you are. I've got this."

Hanging up and putting the phone on silent, she grabbed a

mask from her coat's breast pocket, positioned it on her face, and tiptoed into the alley. As she got farther away from the busy street, she heard hushed voices. Dropping her backpack behind a dumpster, she morphed into a cat and continued forward. No time like the present for a magical recharge.

The potential disaster didn't appear as bad as she'd thought. None of the parties involved looked over seventeen, and the elemental girl held her ground. The lanky blond gang leader drank from a bottle of peach-flavored Smirnoff Ice, which made it impossible for him to appear menacing. "I saw you do your Cherokee Shaman voodoo shit in computer lab. They said it was a power surge, but the sparks came from your hands. Fry the security system, and maybe we won't beat you up."

What type of idiot tried to bully a kid who could summon lightning? This must be nature's way of weeding out the dumb ones.

The girl crossed her arms. "I'm Indian—as in from India, the country in Asia with billions of people. And I'm *Hindu*, not Voodoo. Let me go before I call the cops."

A Miller-Lite chugging ginger sidekick stumbled foreword, reached into the girl's jean pocket, and took her phone. After dropping it on the ground, he broke it with a stomp. Talk about imbecilic, drunk, and wasteful. "I don't care if you don't eat pork. Blast the door so we can get new iPhones."

And what was to stop the girl from "blasting" him? More importantly, how could this possibility not occur to at least one of the five under-developed brains?

Little Miss Smarty Pants, who'd handled the situation with aplomb thus far, jabbed her finger into carrot head's chest. "It's beef, fudge brain. And you can't activate stolen phones anyway. How moronic are you?"

These guys fell into the too-stupid-to-live category. She only stuck around out of concern for the girl's potential PTSD.

Ginger grabbed his victim's wrist. "Do as you're told, bitch."

The kid kneed him in the balls. Howling, he fell to the ground, clutching his crotch. She must have put some power behind that move since the guy's face turned bright red. Sweets doubted he'd get up any time soon.

Turning to face the other four, the girl placed her hands on her hips. "I'm required to issue a warning before I do anything nasty. This is it. Find some other way to get arrested and leave me out of it."

A black-haired goon with a beer gut burped. "What's she talking about?"

She threw her hands in the air. "Urghh...."

At this point, the kiddy gang's drunk alpha reasserted his authority. Grabbing the girl by her waist with one arm, he dragged her to the metal door and shoved her face-first against it. He then proceeded to pour his wine cooler over her head, seemingly oblivious to the white glow emanating from his captive's hands. "Open it, freak, or I'll shove the bottle up your—"

There seemed no time like the present for a nice little telekinetic blast. Launching the boy up in the air and dropping him into a nearby dumpster, Sweets assumed her human form and stepped out of the shadows to face the remaining goofballs. "Two down, three to go. Sure you want to keep playing?"

Liberated, the sputtering mini-witch turned and shrieked, "I'm going to fry your—"

Sweets rushed to the kid's side, grabbed her electrified hands, and pulled the energy into her body in the nick of time. The rush of power almost knocked her out. "Not an expert here, but murder charges don't look good on college applications."

The threat worked. The girl's eyes widened, her jaw dropping such that her mouth formed an O. Then she glanced over Sweets's shoulder. "Look out!"

Foreseeing the blow, Sweets turned and aimed a perfect throat punch at the kid coming at her with a wine-cooler bottle. Dropping to her haunches to avoid his friend's swinging backpack, she swept one leg in an arc and kicked the boy's legs out from under him. As he joined his hacking compatriot on the icy soil, she sprang up to head-butt bozo number three's chin.

For good measure, she pinned all four boys to the ground

with a telekinetic net. "Anyone else?"

"You bitch!" She turned to find their leader leaning over the dumpster's edge, a hunk of black metal gripped in his shaking hand. So the dumb kid had even dumber parents who couldn't bother with a gun locker. Who would've thought?

Before she could whack him with something close by, gale-force winds swept through the alley, launched the kid in the air, and pinned him to the adjacent brick wall. The swirling miniature tornado intensified around the boy until his face turned blue. When his head slumped forward, his weapon disappearing amongst the rubbish, the magical storm subsided and dropped him back into the pile of trash.

A familiar low baritone echoed around her. "Didn't I fucking tell you to wait for me? You could have gotten shot."

Wincing, she turned to face Mikal. Though already elevated from physical exertion, her heart rate quickened from the visual impact of seeing his sculpted form shown off to panty-melting perfection in a black-leather jacket and dark jeans. He'd looked devastating in a suit, but casual garb gave him an oh-so-sexy edge that would make any girl's mouth water.

Then she remembered the more pissed he got, the colder his voice. His quiet reprimand could have frozen lava.

"The thing probably wasn't even loaded," she muttered.

He strode to crouch in front of the petite lightning mage and pulled out a flashy silver badge bearing Enforcement's seven-pointed Elven Star. Though the girl had held her own against five drunken attackers, she'd developed a case of the shakes. Sweets wasn't the only witch wary of the Council. "Hi. I'm agent Mikal Knight. What's your name?"

"A-Alisha Mehra."

He shoved the badge back into the inner pocket of his unzipped jacket. "Are you okay, Alisha?"

She nodded. "Will you lock me up in some Enforcement prison in Cuba?"

When Sweets coughed to cover a laugh, he turned to give her the stink-eye. "Where did you hear something like that?"

"It's all over the Internet," the kid answered.

She tried to suppress the giggles, but they erupted from her nose and came out as a series of snorts. Thumping her chest to dislodge the ball of air stuck in her throat, she pointed at Alisha. "See, it's not just me."

He faced the kid and cleared his throat. "You can't believe everything you read. My car's parked outside."

The girl's big brown eyes welled up.

"I swear I'm not taking you anywhere but home," he ground out. When tears ran down her round cheeks, he lifted his left hand. "Scout's honor."

For some reason, the childish vow worked. Alisha's paling face regained color, and the corners of her lips curved up. "May I please walk? If you tell my parents what happened, they'll never let me go out alone again. It's not fair. I didn't do anything wrong."

Kids, even the kick-ass electricity-wielding kind, could be so damn predictable. Sweets edged around the duo toward her backpack. Grabbing it, she walked backward in the direction of the main street, hoping he'd be too distracted to notice.

A gust of wind hit her hard, shoving her once more into the alley's depths. It didn't stop until she stood a foot away from its creator. Dropping her bag, she crossed her arms and glared at the top of his dark head. "Show-off."

Acting as if nothing had happened, he continued to address Alisha. "You used your powers in public. That's against the rules."

Sweets was pretty certain this fell under the exigent-circumstances caveat, but mentioning the defense might motivate the single Enforcement agent present to lock her up out of spite.

Alisha pouted. "She stopped me before I did anything, and I *totally* issued a warning."

When the kid sent Sweets a pleading look, she nodded to confirm the statement. The teen had followed all the regulations. Left up to her, they would have already parted ways.

Mikal stood. "Your parents and I still need to have a quick chat." As they reached Sweets' side, he took her pack from the ground and slung it over his shoulder. "My...colleague will let them know you acted responsibly and stayed safe, which is the absolute truth."

So much for her plan to rescue and ditch. Maybe mystery one-night-stand dude was running *super* late.

"What about them?" Sweets nodded at the group still squashed to the ground by the power of her mind. "Shouldn't I stick around—?"

He closed his fingers around her upper arm, as if he'd known she intended to bolt as soon as they hit the crowds on M Street. "I'll call in the incident. Once our liaison touches base with Metro PD, they'll round these guys up."

Alisha looked around at the four groaning boys before glancing at the dumpster housing the fifth. "Won't they tell the police what happened?"

"Enforcement has a way of keeping our involvement off the books. Don't worry," he assured the girl as he dragged Sweets along. "After those boys sober up at the precinct, they'll get slapped with underage drinking, drunk and disorderly, and attempted assault charges. If nothing else, their parents will ground them for life."

Chapter Four

Sweets shrugged off her wool calf-length coat and tossed it on the backseat. In honor of tonight, she'd worn a firework-patterned button-down and a blue pleated skirt cut several inches above the knees. The wind chill had forced her to bundle up all day, and if he didn't let her leave soon, Mikal would be the sole beneficiary of her rare effort to dress up. "So, on a scale of one to ten, how pissed off are you?"

Without answering, he started the engine and crossed his arms. His following huff led her to gauge his response at a twelve. They'd parked in front of the Mehra family's low-rise apartment building in Capital South. Though a few minutes' drive from bustling Georgetown, she'd describe the neighborhood as one of the less safe areas in D.C. After talking Alisha's dad out of tracking those boys down and striking their houses with bolts of lightning, Mikal accepted the gift of some colorful, exotic sweets, left behind his business card, and extricated them from the brewing teenage tantrum.

They hadn't spoken a word to each other since leaving the alley. Anger rolled off him in palpable waves, all focused in her direction. While his current mood obliterated the chances of them having sex—the only reason she dared get into his car—the prolonged, disapproving arctic blast gave her goose bumps.

When he continued to pout, she poked his upper arm and

fixed him with her best puppy-dog expression. "Come on. You know I hate the silent treatment. Why are you so angry anyway? What did I do?"

Turning his head, he glared at her through narrowed eyes. "You must have some idea."

She pulled out the elastic holding her ponytail up and shook out her hair. "Umm...no. It's been a super normal day."

"That's the fucking problem," he roared. "You've been playing vigilante for years, and you didn't *tell* me?"

She massaged her ear. "Geesh, can you take a chill pill? Which part are you mad about—my kick-ass ninja moves or my being all stealth-like?"

He banged his fist on the steering wheel, setting off the car horn. "Do you take *anything* seriously?"

"I take a shit ton of things seriously." She scowled. "Stop freaking out and don't be so judgmental. I'm here safe and sound, and I could have handled the entire situation without any help from you." Calling him tonight ranked among the five worst decisions in the past...hmm...couple of weeks at least.

When a few heads poked out of various apartment windows to stare at the single late-model car in a three-block radius, he cursed and pulled onto the street. "This ends tonight, Dulcina. Do you hear me? No more dark alleys or out-of-control mages. You have a vision, you hand it off to me. That's the end of your involvement. You do not put on a stupid mask and play Batwoman. Am I making myself clear?"

"It's Catwoman, and don't talk to me like I'm ten. If it's an option, of course I'll let you deal with it. It's your job, not mine. I don't go around doing this for kicks." And when her visions cut it too close, well.... They'd discuss it later, when he wasn't on the verge of biting her head off.

Buckling her seat belt, she contemplated her options. Talking him down from this hissy fit required sophisticated strategy, bribes, lots of groveling, and more energy than she had at the moment. Logic dictated she sounded a temporary retreat. "Since you're going to be cranky for the rest of the night, can you drop me off at the Castillo? On the off chance my one-night stand is nice enough to still be waiting, I want to give this whole date thing a shot."

For some reason, the statement prompted Mikal to whip his head to face her. "Your one-night stand?"

"Would you please look at the road?" Talk about erratic behavior. To think he'd taught her how to drive. "And yeah. Cat got me this online dating service as a joke—it's how she hooked up with my future brother-in-law. Anyway, it's called Madame Eve's One-Night Stand, and I was supposed to show up at ten. It's almost eleven, so—"

He slammed on the brakes. "Son of a bitch."

Massaging the area where the belt strap had bitten into her right boob, she growled, "Dude, we're in the middle of an intersection. I know you're mad, but double suicide isn't the way to go. Move. What's wrong with you?"

Muttering a string of colorful expletives, he put the car in reverse, backed up, and made a sharp left onto the interstate. With them heading out of the District and across the border to Virginia, she put the chances of her date going through at next to nil. After spending two more minutes traveling down the highway at breakneck speed, she began to suspect their destination might not be her house. She knew him well enough to predict an impending yelling match, and experience warned her it could drag on for hours. The warlock had been on the debate team once, and man could he get longwinded.

She might as well get comfy.

Having spent over half a day in stilettos, her feet were about to fall off. Ignoring her insane driver, she yanked off her boots and slid them behind her seat. Pinching off the socks, she turned around and stuffed them into the side pocket of her backpack, which sat next to her coat. Wiggling her toes, she adjusted the backrest into a slight recline, closed her eyes, and waited for Captain Grouch to begin his opening statement.

A few breaths later, his curt order interrupted the heavy silence. "Open the glove box."

Lifting one eyelid, she turned her head to the side. "Why?'
"Because I said so."

Since she cared quite a bit about worming her way back into his good graces, she bent forward and hooked her finger under the latch. When she spotted a familiar crimson envelope inside the open compartment, her brows drew together. "No f—ing way."

Her hands shaking, she pulled out the vellum invitation. Though too dark to decipher all the text, she got the gist. "Shit fucking hell. You're my date?"

"Don't sound so disgusted."

"I'm not." She took deep breaths. It seemed their future had switched to playing hardball. How had she not seen this coming? "When and why did you sign up?"

"I didn't. It's an undercover op. My boss wanted to make sure there's no mind control going on, which I now know there isn't. That leaves one other explanation."

She clung to her waning belief in the power of chance. "Coincidence?"

He spared her a glance as they crossed the Potomac River. "Do you really think our getting the invitation was an accident?"

She shoved the card back into its original place and slammed the lid shut. "Yup." By the time the night ended, she might just succeed in convincing herself. "But we shouldn't push our luck. Let's make a point to avoid each other...."

He revved the engine, launching them forward even faster. "Is the idea of ending up with me so unthinkable—"

"Of course it isn't," she snapped. "It's so *thinkable* it keeps on happening no matter how many times I stop it. Why do you think I never hang out with you alone anymore?" Once the words slipped out, she pressed the back of her hand over her lips. Maybe he'd missed that little slip?

His eyes turned a lighter shade of gray a split second before he floored the accelerator. The car rocketed past a flashing speed camera before he slowed down. Even in the dark, she could see a miniature storm brew around his pupils. So much for the slim possibility of his hearing impairment.

She'd get into more trouble if she let him stew. Best to talk her way out of this before he connected all the dots. "You *so* got a ticket back there."

"I don't give a flying fuck. How long have you been doing this?"

It might be too little too late, but evasive maneuvers were worth a shot. "I have no idea what you're talking about. What I meant when I said—"

"Don't you dare bullshit me." He lurched onto the side of the road and sent the car to a screeching halt. Turning on the hazard lights, he twisted around to face her. "How long?"

Okay, so that didn't work. She stuck out her lower lip, wrinkled her nose, and commenced slow blinks. "Please stop yelling."

"If you start the crocodile tears, I swear to God I'll put you over my knee and spank you silly."

Despite knowing full well he'd issued an empty threat, the prospect sounded kind of hot. *Focus, Sweets—not the best time to think about kinky sex.* "What could little old me do to a big bad warlock like you?"

He took a deep breath before banging the dashboard with his fist. That must have hurt. "Don't insult my intelligence. For the third time, Dulcina, how long have you been changing our fate?"

She examined her fingernails. "There's no such thing as fate."

"You do *not* want to fuck with me tonight." He grabbed her chin and forced her to meet his gaze. "I should have guessed what you were up to. You've been a manipulative, scheming little witch, and it's my life you kept screwing over. I want to know what you did and why."

"Maybe I just don't like you."

"Try again."

Shaking her head, she pursed her lips and glanced away. For one, not having spent too much thought on her own motivations, she didn't have a good answer. The minor alterations to the timeline had all seemed right at the moment of execution—end of story. But if she told him that, he'd get his panties even more in a wad.

With a grunt, he let go of her, turned off the emergency flashers, and continued down the highway until they crossed into Northern Virginia. "The first time was three years ago, wasn't it?"

His words sent a chill down her spine. The timing couldn't have been a coincidence. Fireworks at midnight started this, and she'd foreseen the same sparks coloring their naked bodies earlier this morning. "There's no first—"

He took a turn too fast, the momentum sending her into the door. "New Year's Eve. Times Square. We were supposed to kiss, but you spilled your drink on my shirt."

"It was an accident."

"And pigs fly."

Her heart thudded as the car careened into a dimly lit park bordering the river. "Are you going to listen to me?"

"Not when I know you're lying. You did it again, three months later, on Easter, and when I came down for Memorial Day, Fourth of July, Thanksgiving, and Christmas. Every time I stayed in D.C., every time you and Shelley visited in New York, something almost happened. But you made up your mind I wasn't good enough."

"Don't be ridiculous. You're awesome sauce—a specimen of male perfection. Why would I ever—"

"You set out to screw some random guy tonight so you wouldn't spend it with me."

She flinched at the combination of hurt and fury behind his accusation. Okay, he had a point there, but that snarling tone was way out of line. She snuck a quick peek at his face. Pissed off might be the understatement of the century.

His hands clenched over the steering wheel as he veered off-road past a wood turnstile. The car came to a jerky stop in a darkened spot by the water. Willow trees bordered them on both sides, the long sweeping vines forming a curtain behind them. Through the glass, she glimpsed the Washington Monument on the horizon. Though she'd never set foot here before, she recognized the view.

Check and mate. Time to concede defeat to Madame Eve.

"How many men have you fucked in my place?"

She swung her head around and gaped at him. "You have no rights over me. *None.*"

Unbuckling his seat belt, he pivoted and captured her shoulders. His eyes had turned almost white; his chest heaved as if he'd run for miles. "How many?"

Her temper already frayed, she shoved at his chest. "Stop acting like a cave monkey. There's been no one, all right? I'm a twenty-one-year-old virgin, thanks to you, so if anyone has a reason to be angry, it's me."

He stared at her in stunned silence. Then his shoulders shook, and he threw his head back with a roaring laugh that seemed to continue for eons.

She stared at the digital clock. If he kept this up for another minute, she'd levitate one of her boots and smack him in the face.

Through shallow chuckling gasps, he teased, "You dicked with our lives for three whole years, and you didn't even get laid?"

And just like that, she had her friend back. Pursing her lips, she fought a smile. He didn't get to ignore her wishes, raise his voice, and make fun of her without suffering some consequences. "I've been busy."

"With what?"

"Getting my damn life together."

He hit his hands on the steering wheel and hooted. "This is so freaking hilarious."

She crossed her arms. "It's my power's fault. All these magical accidents keep messing up my schedule."

"Drop the act." He rolled his eyes. "I know you have the hots for me."

"Do not."

"I've got an invitation from a true matchmaker that says you do."

"There's a chance Madame Eve is a randomized computer algorithm." Not a good chance, but the possibility existed.

Grinning, he settled into the corner between the door and his seat. "Will you admit it already? I'll even say it first."

She glanced at him and remained silent.

"So?" he prompted.

Did he really think she'd fall for that trick? "I'm waiting on you."

"Fine. I want to fuck you—like all the time. So much that I've practically had a permanent boner since I got back. Clear enough?"

The corners of her lips lifted before she could suppress the smug smile. She'd always known, of course, but hearing his confession gave her the warm fuzzies. "Me, too. By the way, you had a weird way of showing it tonight."

"I can be mad and horny at the same time, which reminds me—you aren't off the hook."

Huffing out a breath, she unlatched her belt and mirrored his position. "You're wasting gas."

He pressed a button to open the sunroof before shutting off the engine. Despite the glacial winds outside, the car's internal temperature remained balmy with a steady circulating breeze. She'd bet he saved a ton by never using the heater or air conditioner. Why couldn't Shelley have this power? They needed the cash more than he did, damn it.

Counting off the concurrences between her premonition and reality, she looked up through the open roof and embraced the inevitable. She'd fought change tooth and nail for the past three years. It hadn't hit her until this instant, but she might be ready for it. "So, how do I get off the hook?" Without conscious effort, her voice turned all husky. She might as well wear a neon sign saying, *Fuck me*.

Leaning into the corner, he shifted his seat back all the way and straightened his legs. Though her limbs were much shorter, she followed suit. "Let's start with a confession. Why did you do it?"

She tried to self-analyze, but it had never been her forte. "I don't know why. It felt right each time, I guess."

His gaze drifted to her chest. A gust of wind sliced over it, tearing off the top-most button. She jumped in her seat. "What the hell?"

"Welcome to Strip Interrogation. The rules are simple." Her toes curled at the playful yet predatory gleam in his stormy eyes. Yup, he got her invitation loud and clear. "Whenever you give me a crap answer, I take away a stitch. Any questions?"

She licked her lips. "Is this how Enforcement trained you to question helpless witches?"

He crossed his arms and put on a mockery of a stern expression. "You're the city's vigilante. The gloves come off when there's a badass in the car."

Her cheeks warmed at the backhanded compliment. Placing her hands primly on her lap, she squeezed her upper arms together to better showcase what little boobage she had. When she heard his warning growl, she batted her eyelashes. "What's your question, Detective?"

He bared his teeth at her, but his breath had turned shallow. "Was I right about Times Square?"

She canted her head. "Maybe."

Her next button snapped in half, which meant she'd have to replace all of them. She hated sewing. "Fine. Yes, I did."

"What would have happened between us?"

"I rewrite the future all the time, you know." She lifted her eyebrows in silent challenge. "Always for the better. I wasn't ready for this three years ago. You weren't either."

His narrowed gaze drifted down her torso. The rest of her shirt's fastenings fell victim to his invisible blade in a single swoop.

"Hey, that's cheating." The cotton shifted to reveal her simple black bra. Being pretty-much flat chested, she never bothered with padded underwear. A thin layer of cotton covered her nipples—which had poked out quite a bit. They tingled, too.

She glanced at his large hands, imagined them palming her, and released a ragged breath.

He shifted in his seat. Sneaking a peek at his crotch, she grinned. She knew a boner when she saw one. "You might be right. But I still want to know what you changed."

Lifting one hand, she trailed her fingers down her neck. The tenting around his zipper grew even more pronounced. Interesting—very interesting. "Or what?"

A languid breeze circled her waist and blew upward, its progress tugging her shirttails out from under her waistband. "Be a good girl and do as you're told."

She kept her eyes glued to his. "The crowd counted back from ten." She drew a line along the top of her bra, lingering over her shallow cleavage. "You aimed for my cheek. I turned my head at the same moment." She brought her index finger to her mouth. "Our lips touched." She lashed out her tongue and circled it over the tip. "And you looked at me the way you are now."

If eyes could burn, she'd already be smoke. His chest heaved, the gaps between each breath growing shorter with every intake. "So, why did you pour ice down my shirt?"

She'd asked herself that question countless times. "It was a split-second decision. That version of you seemed so certain...so sure." Dropping her hand, she tried to give him a truthful explanation. "I felt like a cage was about to drop from the sky. I didn't think. I acted."

"Fine. But it's been three years. If I had to guess, you pulled one over on me this morning. You've got to have a theory."

She opened her mouth but didn't manage to get a word out.

"If you try the airhead act, I swear that skirt's turning to scrap. You're flaky, I'll give you that, but most of the ditziness is fake."

Since she had a limited supply of silk-lined wool-blend bottoms, she erred on the side of caution. "Look, by the time today rolled around, botching these visions had become muscle memory. I did it because it's what I always do. If I had to guess...." Uneasy with the confession, she fibbed. "Shelley's my best friend. I didn't want to mess things up by locking lips with her brother."

"Liar."

In a quicksilver move, he lunged forward and captured her nape with one hand. Holding her shoulder in place, he looped his free arm around her waist, splayed his fingers against her lower back, and yanked her toward him. The motion tipped her off balance. With a yelp, she placed her hands on the seat and straightened her arms. The position arched her back, lifting her breasts like an offering. The ends of her shirt drifted down, leaving her exposed from the hips up.

He settled his thumb between her collarbones. "I warned you about the skirt."

The hairs on the back of her neck stood on end. Damn, was that menacing tone sexy. "Any chance we can work this out? I'm running low on winter clothes."

With his free hand, he explored her abs, his fingers lingering on each groove long enough to send a tingle down her spine. His hungry expression more than paid for the hours she'd spent doing crunches. "What do you have in mind?"

Having devoured plenty of inspiring reading material, she had a long list of things she wanted to try. "I'm all stocked up on underwear."

"Fine. But it'll cost you extra." He bent his head and pressed his mouth over the swell of her left breast. With him gripping her nape, she couldn't move away, not even when he sucked hard enough to leave a gleaming coral mark. When he repeated his claim on the other side, she bit back a moan. A fire smoldered at the pit of her stomach and spread to sensitize her skin. Her panties grew damp as he explored her cleavage with teeth and tongue.

He slid his palm along her thigh and under her skirt. Inserting the tip of his finger beneath the side seam of her panties, he flicked it up. With a soft tearing sound, a chilled blade of air sliced the cotton. After repeating the motion along her other hip, he yanked off her shorn underwear and shoved it in his jacket pocket. "I'll keep these."

Covered in a light sheen of sweat, her skin blazed. Her breasts felt heavy, her bra too tight, her parted shirt too restrictive. Her skirt fell over her crotch, the silky brush prompting her to squirm. Part of her wanted him to slice up the rest of her clothing, practicalities be damned.

He traced the underside of her bra with his index finger. Beneath the black cotton, her nipples throbbed. "Last chance, kitty cat. Why did you do it?"

She met his gaze through hooded eyes. "I care about you as much as I care about Shelley. We're too important. I didn't want to mess things up. No kiss is worth two friendships."

"Wanna bet?" Wrapping an arm around her waist, he pulled her against him and fused his mouth with hers. Before she had time to think—before she had time to breathe—he pushed his tongue inside.

She'd foreseen countless variations of this moment. Different times, different places, but always the same man. His hard body surrounded her, his strong fingers circling her nape and spreading over her lower back. She looped her arms around his neck, tilted her head, and let him take over.

His spicy cologne melded with minty aftershave, the intoxicating combination filling her lungs and overloading her senses. Hot, punishing, and relentless, the torment seemed to continue for an eternity. His lips muddled her thoughts; his hands held her prisoner. Again and again, his teeth scraped over her lips, his tongue luring hers into an intimate dance. Weakened and dizzy, she arched her spine as his assault dragged on.

When he relinquished her mouth, she sagged into his hold, her vision blurred and her mind engulfed in a languid haze. "Okay. That was totally worth it."

Chuckling, he brushed his thumb over her cheek, his expression a dichotomy of masculine superiority and shattering tenderness. "Want to do it again?"

She grabbed his collar and yanked hard. "A couple hundred times."

Chapter Five

$\mathcal{D}$ulcina's breathy invitation intensified the red haze obliterating Mikal's sanity. Threading his fingers through her silky hair, he kept her head immobile so he could kiss her the way he wanted. He sucked on her full, luscious lips, drove his tongue into her mouth, and explored every crevice. He repeated the caress over and over, hoping to sate his unquenchable need to touch and taste. They should stop. He should drive her home. A parked car by the river hadn't been where he wanted their first time to be.

But the hunger within him knew no bounds, had no limits. They'd already gone further than he'd planned, with her bottom bare beneath that short skirt, her shirt shorn to reveal smooth, tantalizing skin. He cupped her breast, molding his palm over the thin bra as he drank her moans. With teeth and tongue, she mirrored his every move with eager curiosity, sending his arousal into overdrive. He'd meant for this make-out session to be slow and easy—a teasing dance to give her a taste of what the future had in store—not an inferno that threatened to burn away his control.

Clenching her fingers over the sides of his jacket, she pushed the leather down his shoulders. Surrendering to the madness, he pulled his arms out of the sleeves and tossed the restraining garment to the backseat.

"Hold on." Placing his hands under her knees and back, he scooped her up and swung his legs over the divider, sliding into the passenger seat. Supporting her nape with one arm, he draped her legs across his lap before shoving his hand under her skirt. Fusing his mouth with hers, he cupped the apex of her legs and ground the heel of his hand over her mound. He continued the motion even after he broke the kiss.

Her eyelids fluttered, her head lolled back. "Oh God...."

Pausing to flick on the internal lights, he hiked her skirt up, baring her to his gaze. She writhed on his lap, a blush staining her cheeks as he marveled at the neat, clean-shaven folds. Her shimmying butt pressed his zipper into the ridge of his cock. He groaned. "You're going to kill me."

Ignoring the pain at his crotch, he tortured himself further by parting her plump lower lips. Once he'd exposed her clit, he stimulated the small pink nub with a miniature circling storm of warm wind. Her eyes widened, her pupils dilating until nothing but a rim of light brown remained. When he kept the magical vibration on her, she arched her back, her long, slim legs stretching out to hit the door. One hand clawing at his T-shirt, she bit his chest—hard enough to leave a bruise. A muffled cry filled the car.

"Easy, kitty cat. We're just getting started."

Continuing to hit her clit with a steady current of wind, he yanked down her bra cups to expose her breasts. Though on the small side, the firm golden globes were perfect in their symmetry, their copper tips already poking out to beg for his touch.

Lowering his head, he took one nipple into his mouth, swirling his tongue as he trailed his free hand once more up her thigh. Her shallow pants echoed around him when he intensified the stimulation between her legs, increasing and relenting the pressure in synchrony with his nibbling sucks. He pushed into her tight slit, drawing his finger in and out. Finding plenty of moisture to ease his invasion, he added a second digit.

As he switched over to torment her neglected breast, he

spread his fingers. Her pained yelp prompted him to alter the wind currents so it morphed into a steady, heated pulse over her bundle of nerves, distracting her from his penetration. With her so tight, he'd make damn sure to get her ready. Sucking her swollen nipple past his teeth, he shifted his hand in a languid rhythm. When her inner muscles squeezed, he flicked his thumb over her clit.

"Shit.... I...." " The hand on his shirt clenching into a tight fist, she spasmed. Her spine went stiff. Her bare feet kicked out at the door. Her wet channel clenched and unclenched around his fingers as he continued to stimulate her through the orgasm's aftermath.

When her writhing subsided, she curled into his chest, squeezing her thighs together as he pulled out. Shaking her head as if to clear it, she frowned and muttered, "Fuck me already."

He grabbed her heaving shoulders and pulled her into a seated position. "Not yet."

With an impatient glare, she shifted to straddle him, placing her shaking knees on either side of his denim-clad thighs. Her sweet cinnamon breath grazed over his beard before she kissed his cheek, his jaw, and then the back of his ear. When she drew a circle with her tongue, his breath came out in an audible hiss.

He grabbed her waist with both hands as her lips traced a wet path down his neck. His collar hindered her progress, and she made a frustrated sound before pulling his T-shirt over his head and dropping it on the driver's seat.

Her fingers curling over the hairs on his chest, she licked and bit her way to his pecs, shifting on his thighs so she could swirl her tongue around his nipple. His hard-on turning his jeans into an instrument of torture, he slid his palms up her back and unhooked her bra. Smoothing her shirtsleeves off her shoulders, he wrapped the crisp cotton around his hand until the remaining fabric cuffed her arms. When he pulled, the motion lifted her ass off his lap, making her balance above him on her knees. With her elbows restrained, he guided her backward until her shoulder blades met the dashboard.

Nudging her bra down to band around her ribs, he bent his head and feasted on her breasts, his beard leaving red marks on her dusky skin as he shifted from one delectable mound to the other. Shoving her legs farther apart, he pushed his fingers into her, circling her clit with his thumb until she went limp, her pliant surrender freeing the hand holding her captive. Flashes of red, white, and blue colored her toned abs as he moved down, sucking and biting her flat belly to mark his progress. When he hit her waistband, he bunched her skirt up and shifted to settle his head between her thighs.

"Wait.... It's too...."

Ignoring her whimpered protest, he lapped at her clit, savoring her salty-sweet taste as he continued to finger her. She squirmed against the dash, her thighs quivering when he alternated between gentle sucks and swirling licks, his breath hot against the hard little nub. When he detected the telltale clamping around his digits, he drew his hand back.

Watching her hips undulate in an urgent invitation, a smile curved his lips. He chuckled when he heard her beg. "Damn it. Please.... I'm so close...."

Reclaiming the spot between her legs, he slid his tongue into her, shifting his hand so he could stimulate her clit. She jerked at the sudden switch. A few stabbing licks later, her thighs locked. She screamed.

Wiping his mouth with her skirt, he took advantage of the trembling aftermath of her release to unzip his pants and free his erection. Reaching into the divider to grab his wallet, he unearthed a condom. By the time she opened her eyes, he'd ripped the packet and smoothed it on.

She didn't make a sound as he closed his hands over her hips and pulled her forward. Her inky hair fanned over her shoulders. She shrugged off her shirt and bra. Across the river, more fireworks went off, the bursts of color reflecting over the rippling water. Cradling his face with shaking fingers, she gave him a slow kiss laced with invitation. "Any chance we can finish this before I pass out?"

With a laugh, the last of his concerns dissipated. Splaying his hands over her ass, he shifted her so the head of his cock pressed against her opening. "This might hurt."

She lifted an eyebrow and grinned. "Ya think? You're freaking huge. Come on. Any longer and I'll chicken out."

"Yes, ma'am." Tightening his grip, he lifted his hips and surged into her.

With a gasp, she squeezed her eyes shut. Her teeth clamped over her lower lip. A lone tear fell down her cheek. Moving his hands to cup her face, he wiped the drop of liquid with his thumb. Not moving was one of the hardest things he'd ever done.

She gripped him tighter than any fist. Her naked breasts quivered when she shifted over his length, her hips circling as if in search of a more comfortable angle. As he scrutinized her face for any further signs of pain, her cheeks puffed out, her full lips firming into a stubborn line. With a deep breath, she bent her knees and let her ass drop. Gravity took her all the way down, burying him to the hilt.

"Fuck." His head hit the backrest. All his muscles corded with the effort it took to keep his instincts in check. Twining her arms around his nape, she nuzzled his neck and plastered her naked torso against his chest. When she bit his earlobe, his control snapped. Grabbing her ribcage with both hands, he slid her up his length before pounding into her in hard, pumping thrusts.

Her hair brushed his hands as she threw her head back. She closed her fingers around his upper arms, her blunt nails digging into his triceps. Thought threatened to recede, laid to waste by the gathering storm. But the last shreds of his consciousness refused to accept her silence, couldn't tolerate the slow, pained breaths truncated by high-pitched whimpers.

Holding her steady with one hand, he reached between their bodies. A brief caress was all it took to make her moan.

The soft surrendering sound snapped his leash. He couldn't stop his hips from jerking, his cock from driving into her, but he focused his final scraps of control on distracting her with pleasure. He almost groaned with relief when he felt her relax, when her pleasure-filled cries echoed around them once more. Anticipating his own descent into oblivion, he plucked her clit with his thumb and forefinger, drawing it out as he continued to fuck her hard and fast.

With a keen, she collapsed forward, her trembling descent followed soon by erratic clenches around his shaft. Darkness ate into his vision, consuming all the sparkling colors behind her before exploding in a burst of red.

ᛣ

Kissing Dulcina's closed eyelids, Mikal nudged her naked shoulder. "We need to get going. The sun's coming up."

Murmuring a sleepy inarticulate protest, she snuggled deeper into his chest. His arm had gone numb. Though spacious, the back of his SUV was far from comfortable. Nonetheless, he couldn't imagine anywhere else he wanted to be. "Come on. Do you want the park service to find you butt naked in the back of my car?"

She batted at his mouth, missed, and hit his neck. "Shh.... Five more minutes."

Grabbing her hand, he bit the tips of her fingers. "If you think I'm going to fall for that trick, you're delusional."

When she didn't move, he reached down and pinched her nipple. With a yelp, her eyes popped open. "You'll *so* pay for that."

Pushing her off him and into a seated position, he reached around for his pants. "Looking forward to it."

She rubbed her crusty eyes. "Where the hell are my clothes?"

Pulling his underwear and jeans on, he climbed over the divider to search the space in front of the passenger seat. Victorious in his quest, he turned to dangle the tattered shirt and bra in front of her face.

Grumbling something about wastefulness, she tossed his T-shirt at his head. By the time he shrugged into it, she'd hooked her bra on and shoved her arms into the shirt sleeves. Squinting at him when she fumbled over the nonexistent buttons, she tied the colorful tails under her breasts before pulling on her skirt. With far from graceful movements, she zipped up her boots, the glimpses of bare skin revealed by her struggles giving him an instant hard-on.

When she climbed into the passenger seat, he grabbed her knee. "On second thought, I think we've got some time."

She smacked his hand. "We're out of condoms."

Good point. "I can still make you come."

Her breath hitched, her cheeks turning a pretty shade of coral. "Let's get out of here."

He started the engine. "Since when are you so practical?"

Buckling her seat belt, she settled in and spread her legs, the simple motion turning his morning boner all kinds of painful. He was pretty sure the little minx did it on purpose. "Any later and Shelley will wake up. If she sees me like this—"

"Any reason we're sneaking around? We're both adults."

She scowled. Without an appropriate dose of caffeine, she could be quite the monster in the mornings. "Losing one friend a day to sex is my limit."

Was she serious? Glancing at her peeved expression, he shook his head. Oh, hell. "Don't be an idiot. Friendship trumps sex. Always has, always will. We're just adding...a few fun activities to our joint hobbies."

She sent him a suspicious sideways glance. "We don't *have* any joint hobbies."

He lightly smacked the back of her head. "Stop thinking so much and go with the flow."

She twitched her mouth from side to side. It took significant effort not to pinch her cheeks. "What about this Madame Eve business?"

"Total coincidence." He supported the lie with a firm nod. "Algorithms and all that."

She turned to face him. "So we're like...friends with

benefits?"

If the term helped with her jitters, he could live with it for a few weeks. He stuck out his hand. "Friends with exclusive benefits."

She rolled her eyes. "It's not like I had much of a sex life before this, so fine." Meeting his palm with hers, she gripped fingers and gave him a firm shake. "So what are you doing tonight?"

~A Letter from Tara Quan~

Dear Reader,

Thank you for taking a look at my paranormal series, A Witch's Night Out. I've always been a huge fan of witches and warlocks, and I've had loads of fun creating my own. I keep my stories lighthearted, the angst to a minimum, and the sex just hot enough to make your face grow warm. In all my romances, I aim for a few laughs, handful of clever twists, and a scorching happily ever after.

If I've managed to keep a smile on your face for a few hours, then my goal as a writer is met. I love hearing from readers, so feel free to drop me a line at taraquan@outlook.com.

You can find out more about my other books and various social media haunts at www.taraquan.com.

~Tara Quan

www.ingramcontent.com/pod-product-compliance
Lightning Source LLC
Chambersburg PA
CBHW060149130626
46556CB00006B/2562